Praise for *The SideRoad Kids* Series

"Once again, Kennedy whisks us into the rural past of Michigan's Upper Peninsula. Each evocative story, complete in itself, is also linked to the whole through beautiful prose and memorable characters. Kennedy's deft artistry forges visceral and spiritual connections that define community. The stories run from heart-rending to hilarious. I felt as if I were visiting my own childhood—the secrets, joys, mysteries, and the problems. The entire book stands as a celebration of victories despite brokenness, love despite rejection. *Book 2* deserves high praise and elevates the author to a most honored place among Michigan writers."

—Sue Harrison, bestselling author of *The Midwife's Touch*

"Sharon Kennedy gives us a peek into life in Michigan's Upper Peninsula in the 1950s. It was a simpler, less hectic time when kids like Katie, Blew, Squeaky, and Daisy grew up on farms instead of high rises and used their imagination instead of fancy gadgets to make their own fun. An entertaining read for youngsters. And parents, you might enjoy a nostalgic flashback as well. I know I did."

—Allia Zobel-Nolan, author of *Cat Confessions*

"The stories in *The SideRoad Kids* are often humorous. However, underlying them is a sensitive awareness that being a kid, rural or urban, then or now, is not easy. This is an enjoyable read that will enlighten today's kids about the past and rekindle memories for readers who grew up in the late 1950s."

—Jon Stott, author of *Paul Bunyan in Michigan*

"Over the years, I've read many of Sharon Kennedy's stories. She's an amazing writer who draws you into the lives of her characters and keeps everything relatable. Readers can easily recall similar experiences. She makes you laugh, makes you think, and makes you want to keep reading. *The SideRoad Kids* is an entertaining book about a group of children growing up in Northern Michigan."

—Kortny Hahn, Senior Staff Writer, *Cheboygan Daily Tribune*

"Sharon's stories capture the essence of childhood and growing up in a small community. The antics of *The SideRoad Kids* will keep you entertained and take you back to a simpler time. Some of the stories were published in our magazine and were well received by adult readers."

—Renee Glass, Senior Production Artist, *Mackinac Journal*

"Remember or want to know about the 1950s when girls were playing old maid card games and dolls, disobedient kids were paddled at school and wore dunce caps? Boys were playing with toy guns, dump trucks, plastic cowboys, and catching fish. Country kids were biking for miles, playing in the haymow, bringing cows home for milking, and everyone was playing together. Moms were baking cookies, staying home, and lunches could be served outside in pails.

"In this story, many children face hardships of life while helping each other out—it is realistic fiction. Because they live by Lake Superior in Michigan, tales of ships and sailors are part of the learning at school. Life was exciting every day. Imagination was the most important part of childhood."

—Carolyn Wilhelm, *Midwest Book Review*

"This fine collection of short stories focuses on a group of 6th grade friends in the 1950s living near Brimley, in the U.P. I was a kid in Flint in the 1950s, and if I had read stories like these when a 5th- or 6th-grader I would have been taken aback by the differences in these U.P. kids' lives and mine. Most of the stories are evocative slice-of-life pieces, some are humorous, and quite a few serious and thought-provoking. The stories are honest, believable, sometimes painful, and all capture time, place, and culture with near perfection. A clutch of well-defined, likeable and interesting 6th-grade characters reappear throughout the stories and bind the book together as a whole."

—Tom Powers, *Michigan in Books*

The SideRoad Kids
Book 3
Life as U.P. Adults

Sharon M. Kennedy

Modern History Press

Ann Arbor, MI

ISBN 978-1-61599-828-9 paperback
ISBN 978-1-61599-829-6 hardcover
ISBN 978-1-61599-830-2 eBook

Published by
Modern History Press   www.ModernHistoryPress.com
Ann Arbor, MI 48105   info@ModernHistoryPress.com

Distributed by Ingram (USA/Canada), Bertram's Books (UK/EU)

Also by Sharon M. Kennedy

Fiction

The SideRoad Kids – Book 1: Growing Up in the U.P.

The SideRoad Kids – Book 2: A Summer of Discovery

View from the SideRoad: A Collection of Upper Peninsula Stories

Non-Fiction

Life in a Tin Can: A Collection of Random Observations

The SideRoad Columnist: Observations from an Upper Michigan Author

Contents

An Introduction to *The SideRoad Kids* Series

Book 1, *The SideRoad Kids: Growing up in the U.P.*, introduced a group of lighthearted farm kids. The stories followed them through the 1957-58 school year in the country town of Brimley, a small community in Michigan's Upper Peninsula. Most of the action took place in the classroom or in their homes and revolved around their daily lessons and chores. Humor was an integral part of their lives.

Book 2, *The SideRoad Kids: A Summer of Discovery*, showed the kids beginning to mature and make discoveries that had the potential to change their lives. Readers watched Blew and Flint wrestle with major decisions. Katie and Johnny grew closer, although she wasn't sure if it was Johnny or the bacon from his pigs she preferred. Fenders wrote home, told the kids about life in the Army, and forgave his mother for her strange behavior when he was a youngster. Elizabeth learned to love her stepbrother.

Although the kids were only twelve years old, the summer of 1958 changed them as they passed from childhood to the pre-teen years. They questioned the existence of God. They became aware of the lies adults told them, but not the reasons why. They did their chores, rode their bicycles, fished in the river, played nightly softball games, shared secrets, and grew closer in admiration for and understanding of each other.

Book 3, *The SideRoad Kids: Life as U. P. Adults* is inappropriate for children. The kids are now adults, and each story is told by one character so there is no question as to whom is doing the talking. Some of the boys served in the Army and died in Viet Nam. Others returned home, but the war had changed them. Society had also changed as reflected by the characters. Some married and divorced. Others graduated college and began careers. One joined the Peace Corps. The kids now had kids of their own. Katie, the most independent of the bunch, became a lost soul. Shirley, the most timid, finally escaped the confinement of the gravel road and made peace with her mother.

The first two books are appropriate for young readers regardless of where they live. Whether on a farm or an inner-city neighborhood, the feelings and emotions expressed by the children are universal. They reflect an honest look at life—its challenges, its mysteries, and its discoveries. The kids leave childhood behind in the third book and enter the confusing, contradictory, and often cruel world of adulthood. Their stories will connect with Baby Boomers who lived through the turmoil of seven wonderful, but amazingly bizarre, decades.

Fenders

I slung my duffle bag over my shoulder and stepped off the train at the Sault Ste. Marie depot. The ride from Detroit had been a good one. The travelers on the Soo Line were strangers, but not for long. I was wearing my dress greens, and some passengers asked where I had been stationed. I was lucky. I didn't serve in Viet Nam so nobody called me "baby killer" or any other awful name, and nobody wasted their spit on me to show their contempt. A few youngsters shook my hand. I wasn't ashamed of the time I spent with Uncle Sam. I went from being a no-account country hick in the little burg of Brimley in Michigan's Upper Peninsula to an Army Supply Sargeant. Maybe no great accomplishment in the mind of a CO, but good enough for me. I thought I might become a lifer—a fellow who makes the military his career—but after a dozen years, I'd had enough. Some of the guys who enlisted at the same time I did left after their stint was up. Some spent so much time in the stockade, they were discharged with the same rank as when we finished Basic Training—PFC. It must have been Ma's prayers that blessed me with patience and promotions and kept me out of the war zone or I'd never have lasted as long as I did.

I didn't tell anyone I was coming so no one met me. I didn't mind. It was a beautiful morning. My duffle bag was heavy, but I was used to it. I walked to Ashmun Street. My first stop was the American Café. When Pete, the owner, saw me, he shook my hand and cooked me the best breakfast I'd eaten in a long time. I didn't have to ask for a refill of coffee. My cup was never empty as the waitresses went from one booth to another with a hot pot in hand. People were talking and laughing and enjoying their meal. Everything seemed so normal, so different from the mess halls I was used to. Even the smell of bacon frying in what I envisioned was a cast iron skillet meant more to me than the aroma of Germany's national food, sauerbraten, although it was a pretty close second.

It felt good to be home. As I ate, I heard the whistles of freighters going through the locks. I knew the shops on Portage would soon be opening their doors to tourists. The fudge shops would be busy making the sweet stuff I loved. I paid my bill and walked a few steps to the Karmelkorn Bakery. I couldn't wait to taste their fried cinnamon rolls. Sometimes I even dreamed about them.

I sat at the counter and drank another cup of steaming coffee while I devoured the sweet roll. When I finished, I asked the clerk to put a dozen in a bag for Ma. Then I headed for the door. I was all set to hitchhike to the sideroad when Mr. Sims, one of our neighbors, almost knocked me down as he entered the bakery. I was about to yell at him and tell him to watch where he was going, but the Army had trained me well. No yelling at superiors was a rule I never broke. Sims took a good look at me and stuck out his hand.

"Fenders," he said. "That you? Put it here, boy." He clasped my outstretched hand and wouldn't let go. Anybody looking at us would have thought we were long-lost pals.

"Hello, Mr. Sims," I said. "Yes, it's me. I just got off the 6:45 from Detroit." He finally dropped my hand and pounded my back.

"Who met you?" he asked as he steered me to the counter. "Where's your Pa?" He sat on one stool and motioned me to take the one beside him.

"Nobody met me. I didn't tell the folks I was coming. Thought my orders might change at the last minute. You know how that goes."

"I sure do. It's been a few years since my Wildcat days, but once you work for Uncle Sam, you never take anything for granted. Orders change like the weather, but don't just stand there. Sit down."

"No, I'm ready to get home," I said, but he waved his hand in dismissal.

"How you plan on gettin' there?" he asked.

"Shank's mare until I can hitch a ride," I said.

"My truck's right outside. Sit down while I drink my coffee and eat my cinnamon roll. Bet that's what you came in for."

"You got that right. I tasted them in my dreams."

Sims laughed. "I been to see old man Roi on Sugar Island," he said. "He ain't doing so good. Got a pain somewhere Doc Finlanson can't cure." Sims swallowed the last of his coffee and wiped his mouth with the back of his hand. Then he finished the roll, left a dime tip, and reached for his cap that was stuffed in his back pocket. "Ready?" he asked.

"You bet." I hoisted my gear on my right shoulder and we walked out. "Sure is a pretty morning," I said as we stepped into the sunshine. "I didn't know how much I missed the sound of the freighters' whistles and the call of the seagulls as they wait for whatever the sailors throw to them."

"When you start plowing your dad's fields, you'll have 'em surrounding your head," Sims said. "Nothing can compete with a freshly plowed field as far as seagulls are concerned. I think they'd rather follow a tractor and grab the worms than hang around the freighters and squawk for a free meal, but what do I know. Hop in."

I threw my duffle bag in the bed of his truck and opened the passenger's door. I set the Karmelkorn bag on the seat next to me and rolled down the window. We crossed the Ashmun Street bridge, headed straight up the hill, and on to south US-2. There was no traffic, but that was nothing new. There never was more than a few cars and a tractor on the road at any given time. Sure made a change from the streets of Berlin. They were like Detroit or any other major city. I breathed in the fresh air.

"You know there's been a lot of changes since you left," Sims said. "Some good, some downright awful. I suppose your Ma wrote and told you Johnny Eel hung himself. Poor devil did it right after he graduated high school. Went through the ceremony and shook hands with everyone. I was sitting next to his pa and he was telling me that Johnny was gonna be a pig farmer just like him. When I heard a truck roar down my lane at midnight, I knew it meant bad news. Eel thought Johnny was spending the night with Blew or one of the other boys, but he wasn't. He was swingin' from the haymow rafters. I helped Eel cut him down. I never saw a man so broken. Not even my Wildcat buddies when the shells were flyin' in the war." Sims stopped talking and turned on the radio. I kept my mouth shut and looked out the window.

Ma had written a long letter and told me every detail about Johnny's death. For months I couldn't get the sight out of my head. I couldn't believe he'd taken his own life, not when young boys like him were being killed in Viet Nam. Country boys just like Johnny who'd never held a rifle in their hands unless it was during hunting season. Even then some of the fellows didn't like killing a deer. I met guys so poor they'd eat anything a .22 could bring down, but said they'd never shoot an animal for sport. Ma said Johnny looked real nice in his cap and gown. She said Katie's mother had thrown a party and all the kids were invited. She said Johnny was sad because Katie was planning on leaving the sideroad in the fall and heading down to Michigan State University in East Lansing about a four-hour drive from home. Johnny was cut up about that, but Katie wanted to be an English teacher. Ma said she promised Johnny she'd come home for Christmas and every summer. He'd been sweet on her since they were little kids.

The way Ma told it was that after the party Johnny hung around instead of going home like everyone else. It was getting dark, but he had something on his mind. Katie and Johnny were on the front porch when Johnny took a ring from his pocket and asked Katie to wear it. He told her he loved her, always had and always would. According to Ma, Katie kissed his cheek and promised she'd treasure it forever, but she wouldn't promise to marry him. She said a lot could happen in four years. She might want to live in a city instead of returning home after she graduated college. She said Johnny might find another gal he liked better. She said a whole lot of other things and the more she talked, the lower Johnny's head sunk. Ma said he did everything to stop the tears from coming but come they did.

Katie's mother heard his wails and went to see what was going on. Johnny was on one knee begging Katie to wear the ring until he could afford a real diamond. Ma said Mrs. Clark bit back her own tears at the mournful sounds Johnny was making. She said she knew Katie loved Johnny in her own way, but she also knew Katie was much too young to think about marriage. Viet Nam loomed like a curse over all the boys. Although only Blew and Russell had received their draft notices, Katie knew there was a fair chance Johnny's number would soon come up. Ma said Mrs. Clark wanted

Katie to give Johnny hope, not false hope, but more hope than she had given him. Then when his draft notice came, he would know Katie loved him and would wait for him if he didn't return home in a body bag. Mrs. Clark told Ma all this at the funeral parlor where Johnny lie in his coffin.

"Gonna be a scorcher today," Sims said. "July's been a hot month. Fires in Canada have made the sky hazy for two weeks now. This weather ain't normal for us. I remember the days when summer in the U.P. meant 70-degree weather from June through September. Something's going on in the heavens that ain't natural. You were lucky to be sent to Germany. How'd the Krauts treat you?"

"Not bad. I spent more time on Post than traveling. Went to Berlin a few times and to Dachau. Saw some concentration camps. They were awful." Sims nodded his head.

"What're your plans now?" he asked.

"Not sure. If Pa wants me to stick around, I'll help him with the farm. Ma said he's down to milking only six cows and doesn't keep beef cattle. No pigs either, just a few chickens."

Sims grunted, "You'll find most of the farmers got rid of their milk cows. Unless they put a fortune into new barns and equipment, no dairy was allowed to take their milk. That fellow on Six Mile went big time. He's got to be hundreds of thousands of dollars in debt. Heard he almost got gored by his bull. If it hadn't been for the hay wagon in the field, he'd of been a goner."

"Ma mentioned that in one of her letters. One good thing about having a mother who loves to gossip is she kept me up on all the local news. Even told me about Bell's Brown Swiss cow that was killed by a car on this road."

"News gets around fast when your Ma's telling it. She should of been a newspaper reporter. Course, she tends to embellish a story, but you can't blame her. Her newscasts are more interesting than the paper, and a dang site better than anything on TV." Sims chuckled.

We were by Pine Grove Cemetery and turned right onto the Old Brimley Road. Sims said they don't call it that anymore. They call it Six Mile Road. A few years ago he said they tried to straighten the stretch heading into Brimley, but the county couldn't take out all the curves so it still had plenty of turns although not as sharp as before. It's paved now, too, he said. I looked out the window. "If they dig graves any closer to the pavement, one of these days we'll be driving over the dead," I said. "I never noticed how close they are to the road." I didn't want to hear more about Johnny or any of the kids for that matter. Ma had kept me well-posted, and most of her news wasn't good.

"Only last month I was talkin' to Brown, the gravedigger, and told him the same thing," Sims said. "Brown said the owners plan on buying a couple acres to the west. There's plenty of room behind these plots. As for me, I got my final resting place next to my son on Riverside."

"I didn't know you were married," I said. "Ma never mentioned anything about you having a wife or a son. I thought you were always a bachelor." I was glad the conversation had taken a different turn. Sims put both hands on the steering wheel and began telling his story. I leaned my head against the window I had rolled down an inch and felt the chill of the morning breeze blow through my hair.

"We wed as soon as I got the call from Uncle Sam. I didn't want Margie marryin' while I was gone, and if I died on the battlefield, I knew she'd get a little money from the government. We had a couple weeks together as man and wife. Them was the happiest days of my life. When she wrote and told me she was with child, I was the proudest man on Post. Imagine, me a dad, I kept telling myself. When I got her letter, I knew I'd make it home alive. After basic at Fort Sill in Oklahoma, they shipped us to the Philippines. I didn't see much action there. We were on our way to Japan when we got word the war was over. You should of heard the hootin' and hollerin' coming from the boys. It was too late for the poor devils who were already gone, but for those of us on that ship the news was pure heaven.

"A few months later, I was home. Like you, I didn't tell anyone I was coming. When I walked down the lane and saw Margie sitting on the porch and the little tyke playing with a kitten, I couldn't believe my eyes. I dropped everything and ran like a madman. I swooped Margie and my son into my arms and didn't let go until Margie said I was squeezing the air out of her. What a homecoming that was. We laughed and cried and laughed some more until the sun left the sky. It was only then I ran back for my gear. When she put Stevie in his crib, the kitten crawled in with him. I started to protest, but Margie silenced me, saying they always slept together. Then I carried her to our bed."

Sims stopped talking. I could sense he was no longer in the truck but had left to join his memories. He drove for another mile before he broke the silence. "Margie wasn't what people called a beauty. She was tall and stout and her hands were almost as strong as mine, but she was the only woman I ever wanted. We were a good team. We never quarreled. She used to say that when a man and his wife loved each other there was nothing to quarrel about. We didn't even have what folks called spats. We knew what we wanted, and we worked to get it. When Stevie died from peritonitis we liked to have died with him. Poor little chap. He was only four. He'd been complain' of an ache in his tummy. We thought it was gas and would pass. By the time we got him to the hospital, it was too late. His appendix had burst. There was nothing Doc could do. That was when the light went out of our lives. Margie stopped eating. I started drinking. We stopped working on the house we were building and returned to the old shack that was our first home. We never spoke of Stevie. Three years later to the day, Margie walked into the river. We never found her. Everyone said she'd been washed out to Lake Superior, but I didn't agree. I thought she had sunk like a stone and was layin' at the bottom of that river, but I guess we'll never know." Sims sneezed. "Darn hay fever," he said. "Gets me every year around hayin' time."

I didn't say anything. What does one man say to another when he shares such a story? I knew Sims understood, and I was finally beginning to understand a lot of things. I always thought he was just an ornery old bachelor, but now I knew different. I also knew why he was so broken up when I shot his cat years ago during hunting season. He didn't get mad at me. He just picked up Old Tom and carried him to a shed and said he'd put him in a box and bury him in the spring which is what he did. I know because I helped him.

We passed a dozen small farms and were almost to the sideroad when Sims hit something. He pulled over to see what it was. He switched off the ignition and we got out of the truck. I hoped it wasn't a cat or dog, and it wasn't. What he'd run over was a good-for-nothing porcupine. I hated those rodents. More times than once our dogs had come home with quills in their nose and some in their eyes. When I was six, Pa had to shoot Rowdy, my best pal. That dog followed me everywhere. Sims reached for a shovel in the truck's bed and wedged it underneath the porkie. Then he threw it in the ditch and we got back in. "No harm done," he said. "Sure am glad it wasn't a kid's pet. Let's get you home."

We drove another mile, passed the trestle, and were going by the Wyman farm. My little sister, Daisy, always loved their pink house. Every time Pa drove by, she begged him to slow down so she could study every inch of it. The Wymans were friends with Ma and Pa. One day Pa pulled into their driveway and Daisy was beside herself. She was so excited she could hardly speak when we were invited in. To me, it was just a nice house, but to Daisy it was a pink palace. Funny, how a color can have such a strong impact on a child. I wonder if she's still crazy about pink. When I left for the service, her bedroom looked like a ball of cotton candy.

"They paved Piche Road," Sims said. "Sure is nice driving on something other than gravel. I doubt our road will ever get paved. Too many curves, and the hills are killers. We need a new bridge, but I suppose it'll be years before the county wakes up and puts in a two-laner. The current one's a death trap. Gotta be close to a hundred years old. It can't take the weight of anything heavier than four tons, and people play chicken when they're coming down the hills. Many a time I've pulled over to let some young buck have the right-of-way. I'm in no hurry to meet my doom."

"In one of her letters, Ma mentioned Blew crashed his car into the side of the bridge early one morning when he was coming home after closing the Belvedere in the Soo. She said he wasn't hurt, but he sure sobered up in a hurry. Ma said he walked home and left the car where it hit the railing. At first light, his grandpa got his tractor going and pulled the car onto the road. Blew drove it home. I can imagine the tongue-lashing the old man gave him. He's gone now, isn't he?"

"Yeah, Sullivan died shortly after that. His heart gave out. Left his farm to Blew who never got a chance to run it. Like I said. Lots of changes on the sideroad. You heard what happened to Blew, right?"

"Sure did. Say, where'd that store come from? There wasn't a grocery store here the last time I was home on furlough." I was anxious to change the subject. I didn't want to talk about Blew so when I saw a sign that said "A&B Meat Market," I was glad.

"Abe and Beatrice turned their garage into a market," Sims said. "Opened it a few years ago, and it's a real gold mine. Everybody stops there especially for the meat. It's all local beef and pork. Smartest thing Abe ever did was marry Beatrice. She's got a good head for business. Want to run in and say a quick hello? Weren't you sweet on their daughter?"

I laughed. "That was a long time ago. By now Delores is probably married with six kids. I doubt she'd even recognize me." I was glad the market had taken Sims' mind off Blew.

"Don't be too sure," he said. "She's still single from what I hear. She might be waitin' for you." Sims started to turn into the market's driveway, but I told him if it was all the same, I'd rather get on home. "You're the boss," he said. "But if I was you, I'd start courtin' Delores soon. You'd fall heir to a nice little business if you've a mind to be a grocer instead of a farmer."

"You might be right about that," I agreed. "I never was much for farm work. After being an Army supply clerk, I got used to working inside. Maybe I'll give her a call and tell her I'm home. Test the waters before I get too excited about wearing a white hat and slicing bacon all day." We laughed. Sims wasn't the same man I knew when I was growing up or maybe that was because I'd finally done some growing up myself and wasn't as quick to judge people as I once was.

"Wait 'till you see the river," he said. "Even in this heat, it's higher than it's been in years. We had a hard winter. Broke all records. Snow never stopped fallin' from mid-October right through April. Lots of roofs collapsed, and you should of seen the snow banks. Five feet high if not higher."

We were still on Six Mile near the Burtt place right across from our road. Sims turned left, and my heart beat faster. I was a mile from home. "You can stop here," I said. "Thanks for the ride, Mr. Sims. I appreciated it and enjoyed your company, but I think I'll walk the rest of the way and surprise Ma like you surprised your Mrs. Here, take a couple of these cinnamon rolls. That's my payment for the free ride." I opened the bag, but Sims hesitated. "Go ahead," I said. "I've got a baker's dozen and you know that means thirteen. You'll have a treat to eat with your next cup of coffee. After I get things settled and make the rounds of the relatives, I'll come by your house and lend a hand with whatever you need. Probably won't be until next week."

"That'll be fine," he said. "Thank you, Fenders. I always knew you were a good boy, and I wasn't wrong. You've grown into a fine young man, and I'm proud to shake your hand." He extended his to me. His grip was strong.

"See you soon," I said. I lifted my duffle bag and slipped my arms through the straps. Might as well let my back carry the weight instead of my shoulder. I took my time as I surveyed all that was familiar. Outwardly nothing had changed except the weeds in the ditches had grown taller. I walked a ways and when I got to the bottom of the hill, I stopped on the bridge and watched mist rise from the river. Everything was peaceful. It was past nine now, three hours later than the best time to enjoy a summer morning, but the scene was beautiful all the same. The water was calm. The surface barely made a ripple when I tossed a pebble in. A robin flew above my head and landed on the iron railing beside me. In all my years, I'd never seen one so close. I took it as a sign welcoming me home.

I saw sandhill cranes in the open field to my left and wondered if they were the same ones that returned every year since I was a teenager. There were always two of them, male and female. Like some old married couple, they stayed together until death parted them. I left my post and walked up the hill. Odell's house was just before ours. The boys never finished their treehouse. I met Sam when I was on furlough before being transferred to Ulm in southern Germany. He seemed like a nice enough guy, especially when he apologized for his mother kicking me out of the house after hearing where I was being shipped. I wondered if she was still terrified of Nazis coming for her. Ma wrote that she had spent some time at the mental hospital in Newberry and seems to be doing much better. I hope so. It's a terrible thing to live in the present and be haunted by the past. Took me a long time to understand that.

As I walked on, I heard a horse whinny. Elizabeth was trotting Sunflower towards me. Both girl and horse had beautiful strawberry blonde hair that looked all the more lovely as the sun hit it. Elizabeth was a flirt. She threw me a kiss and asked me to stop and tell her all about the Army, but I just waved and walked on. I was about to turn in our driveway when I heard the roar of a hotrod tearing down the hill and aiming straight at me. When he saw me, the driver slammed on the brakes. I was surprised there were any.

"Fenders, is that you?" Squeaky yelled. He and Flint jumped out of the jalopy. "You've put on some weight," he said. "You look like a real soldier instead of a bean pole. Put it here, Pal." He shook my hand and pounded my arm. He'd added extra pounds to his short frame, too, but other than more padding around his middle, he looked the same except for a thin layer of hair underneath his nose that I guess he called a mustache. Flint had grown at least another foot and had filled out across his shoulders. His blond hair was as long as a rock star's. He grabbed my hand and pumped it.

"Man, you look good," he said. "Did you bring home a pretty Fraulein? Where is she? Did you bring one for me? Did you know I made it out of Nam with nothing more than piece of shrapnel in my left leg? Did you know I left a piece of my little finger in the Mekong Delta? Are you home for good this time?" Flint peppered me with questions.

"All in good time, Flint. I'll answer all your questions in good time, but now I'm going to walk into Ma's kitchen and surprise her. She's not expecting me." We shook hands again and the boys got back in their rattletrap. Squeaky blasted the horn. They waved and were gone in a cloud of dust. Ma must have heard the commotion because the screen door opened, and she stood on the porch. "Ma," I yelled. "It's me." She looked like she was going to faint. "It's really me, Ma. I'm home for good." I ran towards her, jumped on the porch, and hugged her like there was no tomorrow. Unlike the poor lads who would never see another one, I knew plenty of tomorrows lay ahead for me.

Candy

Nobody told me I'd lose my mind before I was thirty. Nobody ever told me a goddamned thing of importance. It was up to me to find out how things worked inside and outside my head. The train in my ears got so loud I used to think the noise would drive me crazy with its incessant ringing and humming and buzzing like some unearthly being was howling to be let out of prison but there was no jailer with a key so there was no escaping the screaming that refused to be muffled. I tried everything. Nothing worked except turning the dial on the radio—with the old glass tubes cutting in and out without any warning—as high as it would go to drum out the cacophony between my ears but even that didn't dissipate the volume. It only changed the frequency from a red screech to a dull monotonous gray.

Sometimes I wondered if the other rats in the maze of this odd thing we call life were tormented by a train in their heads or is head singular I'm never sure for although each rat has only one head when I use "rats" it seems to me I should also pluralize "head" but that doesn't make sense either because regardless of the number of rats in this hellhole we call life each of us as far as I know is—thankfully—cursed with only one head and two fleshy apertures on each side we call ears. Well? Do the other rats hear what I hear? If not why not?

When I was a little girl say around eight or nine I awoke one summer night to a banging sound and called to Mother. She came quickly and I asked her what that noise was but she didn't hear it so I begged and pleaded in my childishly pathetic way and she went downstairs and investigated. When she returned to my bedside and said there was no noise I could still hear it and it was not inside my head. It was outside. I didn't know where but outside in the dark night something was banging to be let in. Mother turned off the light and crawled into bed with me and held me reassuring me the noise would go away and maybe it did when sleep overtook me I don't remember but I remember Mother snuck back to the bedroom she shared with Father as soon as I slumbered.

Throughout my teen years Mother sold Avon when Daisy's mother quit and handed Mother all her brochures and customers. Although she would never admit it she felt superior to the other women on the dusty gravel sideroad where we lived. I hated feeling different from the other girls. They thought I was perfect but I knew better. I knew they envied me because the house I lived in was a castle compared to some of the shacks my friends called home but that's what theirs was—a home—which is something the place where I spent eighteen years was only a house filled with pretty things Mother bought from fancy catalogs and Cowan's Department Store. She drank tea and ate delicate pink cakes after she had lined up an army of products to show her customers. She enjoyed her refreshments as the ladies thumbed through a brochure looking for whatever they could afford when they knew perfectly well they couldn't afford anything. Maybe Elizabeth's mother maybe even Katie's but certainly not anyone else's ma not even Daisy's who had stashed away enough creams and lotions and colognes and lipstick samples to last a lifetime.

I met Toby one month before I graduated high school and received a scholarship of three-hundred dollars that my parents expected me to use when I attended the Soo branch of Michigan Technology University located in Houghton a town about a four-hour drive west of Brimley. I had no intention of going to college but I accepted the check and thanked our principal who was an old man or at least looked like an old man in my young eyes that were filled with stars because I had fallen in love with Toby Willis of Alabama or Arkansas or Mississippi or one of those other backward southern states but I didn't care because Toby was my ticket out of my hick town. As soon as his father was transferred to another Air Force base out of Kincheloe in Chippewa County Toby promised I was going with him. I couldn't wait.

Mother hosted a graduation party meant for me but really it was her way of showing off our mansion and perhaps making a few Avon sales. She invited the Marquette relatives and some rich friends from the Soo and a sprinkling of other old people I had never met because they lived across the St. Marys River separating Soo Ontario from Soo Michigan. The women dressed in pastel colors like all old women dress to make them look young and fashionable even with gray hair that has a tinge of blue in it and old watery eyes red around the lids and buckets of cheap cologne splashed behind their ears that nearly choked me when they put their arms with loose flesh around my slender firm shoulders belied their age. I pretended I didn't mind. Toby wasn't invited but that didn't bother me either because I knew I would sneak out of the house when Mother and Father and our two dogs Sniff and Snuff were asleep. I was excited. For the first time in my life I was going to do something I had dreamed of doing for no better reason than rebellion. I was going to disobey my parents. Had I known that simple act of insurgence would lead to years of miserable misery I would have stayed between my clean white sheets with little pink and white flowers embroidered around the edges of my pillowcases and stayed in my own bed where I belonged instead of in the back seat of Toby's Ford Fairlane an old man's car driven by a son whose father was a bigshot. Toby borrowed the car without permission and smashed it as he was coming down the hill near my house because he was drunk and I had lost my virginity earlier that evening.

Toby was afraid his father would force him to enlist and do his duty to his country and maybe get killed in Viet Nam or Laos or Cambodia or some other country in Southeast Asia but duty and death were the last things on Toby's mind because there was only one thing he was interested in and that was sex with a pretty little gal who had never done more than hold Flint's hand or allow him to kiss her cheek. I knew girls who had to get married. Mother said they were bad and she was glad I wasn't one of them. I was glad too but when Toby kissed me and I got a strange feeling where it matters most I understood why those bad girls did bad things and I didn't think about the consequences because consequences were the last things on their mind as the handsome young boy on top of them pulled down their panties and slipped his hard thing I didn't know the name of into the secret slippery mysteriously moist opening between their legs and begged for more. We were married in July and the train in my head felt like an explosion as I walked down the aisle of Brimley's St. Francis Xavier Catholic Church dressed in white and wishing I had never met Toby or his instrument of pleasure or his father's Fairlane that would lead me to God only knew what.

Missy was born seven months later. It was a bright February morning. The thirty-six hours of labor almost killed me but when the nurse handed Missy to me and said I'd done a fine job I forgot about the pain that had torn through my body and ripped it open. I even forgot about the screaming in my ears and the husband who was not by my side but still in our bed in his parents' house where we were allowed to live so long as we kept our clothes on and my shame hidden until a proper explanation could be thought of to quiet the wagging tongues of his father's kin although they didn't give a toss when the baby arrived earlier than expected because they knew it would because why would a Northerner marry a Southerner when everyone south of the Mason Dixon line was still fighting the Civil War unless she was with child like all the Southern belles were? Toby's father had retired and moved back to his birthplace Oxford Mississippi.

Toby was a disgrace to his old man because he tore up his draft card when his number came up. He wanted to return to the Upper Peninsula and take the ferry to Canada and hide in the Yukon Territory or Saskatchewan or some other Godforsaken place where the American MPs or Canada's RCMPs would never find him but his father said no. That's when Toby decided to register at Ole Miss if they'd have him which they did so Toby was safe at least for awhile while other young men including some of my classmates were coming home in body bags but none of that mattered as I looked at Missy with a tuff of red hair on her beautiful little head and counted her tiny fingers and toes reassuring myself they were all there and pressed her to my breast and nourished her as my Mother had never done with me because she said my sucking was too painful on her tender nipples. She had come for the birth and stayed with me as I screamed for thirty-six hours and begged the doctor to cut me open and take away the pain and the kid who was causing it but Mother said it wasn't normal to be cut open for no other reason than I hurt. I squeezed her hand until my fingernails cut into her soft pink flesh that had never seen a day's work and looked as lovely as those of the hand models in her Avon brochures. She let go when I drew blood and was almost willing to ask the doctor to honor my request and cut me open but changed her mind when the pain I had inflicted upon her began to ease. She and Father drove back to Michigan later that evening after the nurse convinced her surgery and stitches would not be required and the damage I had inflicted upon her hands would heal and very likely not leave scars that any of her customers would notice. Mother expressed her thanks by handing the young woman a brochure and a small white plastic tube of Crimson Red lipstick she had pulled from the enormous white plastic purse dangling from her left arm.

Toby showed up three days after the birth. He said he had to attend classes or lose his student deferment but now that he was a daddy maybe he could skip classes altogether because now there was no need for a university degree and Ole Miss could go to hell with their integration policy messing up everything and Negroes sitting next to him and breathing their black germs on him when everyone knew Ole Miss was off limits to their kind when Hampton College was eager to increase their enrollment and wasn't that far away in Virginia and why didn't the uppity Negroes go to Hampton if they felt it necessary to learn something other than how to pick cotton eat watermelons fry chickens and walk barefoot down dirt roads. Toby liked Missy right from the first. Doted on her when I brought her home in that stinking Ford Fairlane that was almost rusted out from all the salt spread on the U.P. roads. Doted on her until the next one came along the next year. Dotty was her name.

Things got worse after she was born. Instead of beer Toby started drinking the hard stuff telling me it was the only way he could cope. Cope? What did he have to cope with? His parents paid all the bills. His mother helped with our girls. They were sweet babies. It was easy to tell she adored them her first grandchildren. It didn't matter to her that I was a Northerner and maybe my great-grandfather had fought against one or more of her relatives in the only war that Southerners were interested in that being the one fought between the states and called Civil because that was all in the past now and nothing matter anymore except the future and what it would bring for Missy and Dotty. What kind of future they would have with a drunken father and a Northern mother but she was kind to me in spite of my roots I had no say in because where you land is not up to you when you're born.

A couple times I left Toby and took the Greyhound Bus back to Michigan back to the sideroad. The first time was a few months after Missy's birth. Mother wanted to see her again but she didn't have the energy to travel back to Mississippi so I got on the bus at Holly Springs and rode it to please her. Fenders was on some sort of leave from the Army and we shared the same seat and it was hot in the bus because I learned very quickly that Southern people are always cold if the temp drops below 80 degrees F inside or out. My legs kept sticking to the plastic seat and every time I moved Fenders laughed because my legs made a disgusting sounding noise. I laughed too and even Missy who knew nothing about humor giggled or gurgled right along with us which made us laugh harder and made the long trip more enjoyable than it was miserable. Fenders didn't ask any questions that might have been embarrassing to me and my plight although he didn't know I was in what could only be called a plight and for that reason it was easy to talk to him and explain that things weren't always as they had seemed when I was young and everyone thought I was spoiled although I wasn't a brat because I wanted the kids to like me and I knew they wouldn't if I acted like one.

When Missy cried Fenders offered to hold her. He cooed just like Blew did when Mr. Clark bought the piglet from Johnny's dad and the little pig was scared so it ran back home and the next morning Mr. Clark and Katie brought it back to its new home and Blew walked into the old chicken coop no longer used for the chickens but for JEP as Katie called him which stood for Johnny Eel's Pig and Mrs. Clark was holding it and Blew stroked its prickly hair and JEP settled down just like Missy did when Fenders held her and I fell asleep with my head on his shoulder until the Greyhound pulled off US-72E and stopped at a little town near Nashville and the driver said we had ten minutes to stretch our legs and use the restroom which cost a dime. I changed Missy's diaper and handed her to a kind woman with a Southern drawl who called me dearie and held the stall door open so I didn't have to pay the dime the toilet demanded. I left my pee in that clean toilet and washed my hands and the sweet lady handed Missy back to me as I knew she would and we got back on the bus. Fenders was waiting for us and offered me an egg salad sandwich he had bought from a machine and it was good.

The farther north we traveled the colder it got because even in May there were still little patches of snow as we traveled through back roads with no road signs telling us what the road was called much like our old sideroad had no name just a rural route number which meant nothing to city people who had names on every street corner so city folks could find their way to wherever they were going and not get lost not like in the country where people gave directions by saying Now if you go straight as the crow flies about a mile east and make a sharp left at the elm tree that got hit by lightning during the storm of '37 you'll see the old Mac place with the barn sporting a corrugated metal roof the dang fool put on when every other farmer shingled his roof but Mac was right the metal outlasted the shingles by a good fifty years if not longer then turn right just past the fencepost with the red Hills Bros. coffee can overturned on it that marked a good blueberry patch but the berries are all gone now and drive a few minutes more you'll be at the place you're looking for. Our Detroit relatives hated coming to visit because there were no street lights and at night everything was blacker than tar and my aunt was never sure where she was going and her husband was always mad because she usually missed our road and drove past the railroad tracks and over the Brimley bridge and almost to Horsefeather's General Store near Bay Mills before she realized she was a good ten miles away from our place. My uncle never drove a vehicle in his life and never let my aunt forget she was by far the worst driver he had ever had the misfortune to travel with. When he was old and senile she punched him. He went down still yelling about her terrible driving and then two months later he died and she felt guilty so she cleaned her house and put on her best dress and Sunday hat and shot herself.

We locals didn't care. Some of us had an outside light we flipped on when we heard a car come down our lane or turn in our driveway but more often than not we never bothered with the light because Father was always feuding with the REA and telling them their rates were too high and he didn't give a twit about their mascot EverReady so the outside light was kept off until the Detroit relatives were pounding on our screen door and yelling to be let in. Fenders agreed the REA was awful expensive. He told me his ma permanently kept the kerosene lamp on the kitchen table because it came in mighty handy when the lights went out which is what they did quite often. He fell asleep as I looked at my reflection in the window instead of at the stars beginning to sprinkle the sky because it was night. All I could see was myself a young girl holding a sleeping baby sitting next to a handsome young man in uniform. We looked like a happy family and I wished it was Toby sitting next to me but I knew he'd be sitting on a bar stool in one of the dark dingy bars around Holly Springs with some floozy rubbing his thighs just like I used to do until I landed with Missy who I love with all my heart and wouldn't trade for a full bushel of black walnuts even if someone offered one.

I hadn't actually gone off Toby. I was just tired. Life in the South was a whole lot different from what I was used to. Fenders noticed I didn't talk like my old self. I blamed my new speech on that Southern drawl. When I met Toby my heart melted at the sight of his blue eyes the color of Lake Superior on a clear day but when he said howdy in the way only a Southern boy could say it I was smitten. I fell in love with that drawl long before I fell in love with Toby and to this day I don't think I'm in love with him only with his voice. Even when he's mean to me due to the drink that drawl can talk me around. In the beginning I'd ask him to talk—to say anything even the alphabet—just so I could put my chin on the palm of my right hand as I leaned on our kitchen table and into him and listened but after awhile that drawl dripping from his mouth like honey from a beehive started getting on my nerves. Like eating too much honey can make you sick so too that drawl was too sweet for my liking and I began to sour on it. Toby didn't notice his charm had worn thin until my belly was so big with Missy I couldn't stand his voice let alone his touch and for the first time ever I screamed at him to shut his goddamned mouth and keep it shut.

I must have slept. When I awoke it was morning and Fenders was holding Missy and the driver had pulled into a Greyhound station in a place called Central City. We were given another ten minutes to do our business. I breathed a sigh of relief when a roadside sign said we were on US-431N. Fenders said we still had a long way to go what with the bus stopping every thirty minutes or so in some little burg where a few folks got off and another few got on. A lot of Negroes rode the Greyhound. I had never seen one prior to leaving Brimley so I didn't feel one way or the other about them. Fenders said he had met plenty in the Army. He said they were just the same as us only they could dance a whole lot better and usually saw the funny side of things. He said one six-foot-tall Negro helped him get over his nerves when he enlisted. He said the fellow was as young as Fenders but he was street smart because he learned the ways of the street long before he quit school at sixteen. He said regular schooling was fine for white folk but for people of black skin it was mostly a waste of time because all the Southern boys he knew were heading North to work at a car factory in Detroit if they didn't get a job in Chicago first and book learning was not a requirement for getting a job on the line.

I enjoyed looking out the window as we passed farms and pastures and people going about their business. The bus was quiet except for an occasional cough from the young man behind us who smoked one cigarette after another. He apologized if his cough was disturbing Missy but I said no that she could sleep through almost anything until she got hungry. The man laughed and said he was originally from Memphis but couldn't get work there so he turned to hoboing. He said there was no pay in it but as he had no home and no address the government couldn't track him down and send him to that Asian war that was none of our business where a couple of his buddies had already been killed. He said the government was lying to us and that it wasn't just a few advisors over there but a whole slew of armed troops and he didn't aim to be one of them. He said poor dead President Kennedy had been a good man but he couldn't buck the Pentagon who forced his hand and made him send nigh on to twenty thousand of them advisors turned soldiers and he wasn't having any part of it. He said it was too bad Oswald or whoever it was that really shot him hadn't waited a few years and maybe Kennedy could have sorted out the mess and there wouldn't be no undeclared Viet Nam War raging today. Then the boy leaned back and lit another cigarette. He couldn't have been more than nineteen but he looked fifty.

Fenders and Missy slept then woke then slept some more. I tried to keep my eyes open so Missy wouldn't slip from my arms but I was tired too. Fenders held her while I leaned my head against the window and closed my eyes. I burrowed into the fake fur collar of my coat and dreamed of home—not Toby's parents' home but my real home. I was so homesick I dreamed about my lovely yellow bedroom with the frilly lampshade covering the yellow lamp on my nightstand and the blue clock radio next to it. I loved that lamp and radio and wanted to bring them with me but Toby had so no so I left them behind. Now I was glad I had. I knew Mother would have left them and everything else exactly as I had left them because she knew I'd be back maybe not for good but for sure I'd be back. I saw the movie magazines I loved all piled in a neat corner of my closet. I always put the latest edition on top of the old ones so I knew exactly where to find it when I wanted it.

Everything in my room was neat and tidy. That's the kind of girl I was. I've changed in that department because when you live with people who are a bit on the sloppy side that's the way you become because otherwise you'll drive yourself nuts if you're constantly picking up after everyone. I thought Toby's dad was a bigshot at the air base but he wasn't. He wasn't even in the Air Force. He was just a civilian who landed a job nobody else wanted. He was a janitor and so cheap he even brought home whatever he found in the wastebaskets if he thought he might one day use the bits and pieces of paper or half-smoked cigars in the ashtrays on an officer's desk. I didn't know what I was getting into when I got into it. If I hadn't stopped at the Midtown Restaurant on Ashmun Street in Sault Ste. Marie and ordered a chocolate malt I never would have met Toby or his drawl or his father's Ford Fairlane's backseat and would still be sleeping in my pretty bedroom with the frilly lampshade over the yellow lamp or selling Avon with Mother and winning prizes and married to Flint who adored me but didn't have a drawl or a blue Ford Fairlane with a big back seat. Missy started crying. I awoke from my daydream as Fenders handed her to me and said he thought she needed changing.

We were almost at the Michigan border when all traffic stopped due to a freak spring snowstorm around Fort Wayne. We waited in that bus until the tank ran out of gas and the driver called for another bus. It was hours before it could get through the snow and traffic. For the first time since her birth I was glad Missy nursed. I had a full supply of milk. Fenders was ever the gentleman and read a magazine whenever I put Missy to my breast which I kept well-covered by throwing a soft pink receiving blanket over her. When the plows finally cleared the roads and the cops cleared the car pile-ups it seemed the driver took every dirt road he could find to avoid another freeway pile-up. We had changed buses at Fort Wayne—don't ask me why because one bus was the same as the next—but we changed and this bus did seem a bit warmer than the last. Ninety degrees at least.

"Your ma will be happy to see you," Fenders said.

"I hope so. I called her just before Toby drove me to the bus station. She sounded excited."

"Candy, are you happy?" he asked.

"To tell you the truth I don't know. Everything happened so fast—getting into trouble then getting married and moving to Oxford then giving birth—that I haven't had time to think whether I'm happy or unhappy or what I am."

"Then you must be happy otherwise you'd know for sure that you're not."

"Is that how things work?" I asked. "I never thought about happiness when I was young. I just did what the other girls did. We played dolls and got into Mother's Avon samples. Then in high school we were cheerleaders and it was great fun riding the fan bus when we played the other basketball teams. Remember how we always laughed when we played Detour or Cedarville because we knew those teams were easy to beat, but we didn't like Rudyard because they had too many good players?"

"Sure I remember," Fenders said. "Basketball was about the only thing I was good at. I sure wasn't much of a scholar. It's a wonder I ever graduated. I was dumb."

"You weren't dumb. You just didn't like school. At least you didn't quit. You stuck it out which is more than I might do with my marriage. I wish I was still single." Without meaning to I started crying. Fenders patted my hand and took Missy from me as I fumbled in my purse for a Kleenex. "I'm sorry. I didn't mean to cry."

"Everybody cries when they're starting something new, Candy. And that's what you're doing. I cried when I left home for Fort Carson. I didn't have a clue what was going to happen, but things turned out okay. You go right ahead and cry. I'll entertain this little lady. She sure is a pretty baby. She has your blue eyes and long eyelashes, and I see a tinge of red in her hair."

"She has no hair, silly. Just a little bit of fuzz on her head." We laughed as tears ran down my cheeks.

"Looks like hair to me. She'll grow up to be a beauty like her mother. You'll need a stick to chase away all the boys. Look, we're in Michigan. We'll soon be home."

"I can't wait to get off this bus. I'm sure Father will meet us at the station while Mother puts the finishing touches on the homecoming meal. Who's meeting you, Fenders?"

"Nobody. I didn't tell anyone I got leave before being shipped to Germany."

"Then it's settled. You're riding with us." Fenders thanked me and went back to reading his magazine. I leaned back in the seat. Missy snuggled her head underneath my chin. I closed my eyes and mentally counted the miles until I fell asleep. Then I heard Fender's voice.

"There she is," he said. "The Mighty Mac. Won't be long now, Candy. Won't be long now."

And it wasn't long either not back then when Missy was only three months old and Dotty hadn't arrived yet but this is 1974 and everything's different now. This time I'm not on the Greyhound bus. I'm driving the Fairlane straight through to Michigan and hoping we'll make it because if we don't Toby might catch me if we have car trouble and have to stop at a motel while the car's being repaired or worse yet if we have to phone Father and ask him to come get us if I don't have enough money for both the repairs and a motel room.

It's the endless drive on the freeway that pulls the memory of Fenders and that bus ride so long ago to the forefront of my mind. It seems like it must have happened to another girl not me not the once-pretty redhead who was popular with everyone because no one knew how she really felt about anything. I always followed Mother's advice and kept my heart well off my sleeve. Keep your feelings to yourself was her last advice to me as Toby honked the horn on our wedding day eager to be away from Brimley and the prying eyes of relatives and classmates. Smile and be pleasant no matter how upset you are. It's not nice to let your in-laws know you're sad or angry or anything except that you're happy to be living with them. Treat everyone the same. Whether his kin are rich or poor never look down your long nose at any of them or his kinfolk will think you're a Northern snob. You don't want that do you as you enter your new life as a wife and mother?

So I took her advice and kept my mouth shut all the while as the storm in me was brewing like the tea kettle Mrs. Willis was so proud of because it was a relic given to her by an uncle on the Willis side who had given his left leg while defending his cotton fields against the invaders from the North. She thought more of that tea kettle than she did of Mr. Willis. It was easy to understand why. He wasn't much good for anything other than leaving the impression of his body in the chair he rarely vacated except to pull another chair up to the supper table and eat until he got tired of chewing and flipped his plate over and asked if Mrs. Willis had baked a custard pie for dessert. I didn't blame him either because she wasn't an easy woman to live with but Mother's words echoed in my ears along with the siren running through them so nobody knew how I felt about either of them or any of the other in-law aunts that came calling every day as regular as the wind-up Westclox that was a wedding present for Mrs. Willis and was placed with great pride on the best piece of furniture she owned that being the mahogany buffet that held her underclothes instead of table linens. The green-checked oilcloth was good enough for that. The truth would have landed me in their baptismal waters until I had repented of all ill-will I felt towards them and their kind although I had been baptized into the Catholic Church as an infant of six weeks in case I caught some terrible disease that threatened to take me from Mother and this earth. She would have blamed Doc Hubbard if he hadn't been smart enough to cure me.

The girls were getting restless. I stopped at the Gaylord exit thankful the Fairlane was still running good. We'd be home before sunset if there was no road construction. Missy and Dotty would be sleeping in my old bedroom left just as I had left it because Mother didn't want to change anything so nothing changed. She might have put a new light bulb in the yellow lamp with the frilly yellow lampshade or she might have left the old 60-watt bulb in because it had stood the test of time so there was no point in throwing it away when she no doubt assumed there was plenty of good wattage left in it.

I topped off the tank. Pumped the gas myself something I never dreamed I'd ever learn to do but in the past years I had learned to do a lot of things I never dreamed of doing like throwing a few things in one suitcase grabbing my girls and sneaking out of the house while my husband and in-laws and the four hounds they kept were still deep in a drunken sleep or simply too lazy to see what was going on or to bark.

"Hurry, girls," I said. "It won't be much longer now." They came running as I knew they would because they're good little girls like I used to be before I met Toby and his blue eyes and Southern drawl and this goddamned Ford Fairlane that turned my safe world upside-down.

Elizabeth

"Momma, will they ever stop coming?" I asked. "Did Captain know everyone in Ontario as well as the Upper Peninsula?" St. Francis Xavier Catholic Church in Brimley was practically bursting at the seams. It was the hottest day ever recorded on this date. If any more people squeezed into the small church, Captain wouldn't be the only one laid to rest. Heatstroke would claim at least another half-dozen of his friends. I stifled a laugh.

"Shush, Elizabeth. We must keep up appearances. Your stepfather was a much loved and admired person. Think how proud he would be if he could see the crowd." Momma's lips stretched into a thin rubber band of pink as she hid a polite smile behind her lovely black lace gloves that reached all the way to her elbows. The man she had married twenty-six years ago would soon be nothing more than a memory, and Momma would be a very rich widow. Whenever she went to a wake, she would tell the person sitting next to her that it was much better to marry a man at least twenty years your senior. There was a good chance he would die first and leave his wife well-provided for. Today was proof positive of her good fortune, although she would rather eat roadkill than admit it.

OMG, I'm talking like Flint Flanders. That's what living in this backwater town has done to me. Flint's on the other side of the aisle. He'd roar with laughter if he could read my mind. I used to be such a little lady. Momma dressed me like a Christmas tree and paraded me everywhere so people could admire the girl who was a beauty destined for great things. And I did do great things. I got sued in Chippewa County Probate Court because some jealous bitches wanted to see me swing from the nearest elm tree. Thankfully they all died in the 1950s when the blight killed them so I escaped the hanging, but not the gossip. It wasn't my fault that nice old Mr. Sims died last year and left all his money and chattel to me. I hadn't asked for it. I was happy to buy his groceries and drive him to his various appointments when he could no longer drive himself. He had always been kind to me so when he needed help and no one stepped forward, I did. I thought it was the least I could do for any person who was old, alone, and lonely. If Mr. Sims had known all the trouble his gifts were to give me, I believe he'd have burned the whole lot and cheered as everything went up in flames. Had I known, I'd have cheered right along with him.

"Captain was a wonderful man and a friend to all," Father Munch was saying. "He never missed Sunday mass or Holy Days of Obligation. He was a pillar of obedience during the Lenten season. He paid for the kneeling pads most of you have your shoes on right now. He rewired the sacristy. He was a giant among men. Who would like to step forward and give a tribute befitting such a great man?" The church was so quiet I could hear the sweat dripping off Mr. Eel sitting behind me. "Come now, folks. Don't be shy. We're all friends here. Come, step forward and say a few words." Still, no one moved. Either their rear ends were stuck to the pews or they were too honest to tell the truth. Finally Ronnie, my stepbrother, left our pew and walked the few steps to the altar. Momma gasped and tried to grab the hem of his black jacket, but she was too late. Ronnie cleared his throat.

"Friends, neighbors, loved ones," he began. "Father Munch said some mighty fine things about dear old Captain, most of which were true. But you know as well as I do that the man resting peacefully in the coffin next to me was more than a good friend and a good Catholic. He was a saint." Ronnie's brown eyes drilled into Momma's. Her black veil covered most of her face, but I could feel it flame red. I'm sure Ronnie could, too. We had no idea what he was going to say next. Momma hadn't been thrilled when at the age of six his mother and Momma's first husband—my Daddy—had dropped Ronnie off at our house for what was supposed to be the summer but ended up being two decades. He had grown into a fine young man, and I was proud of him, but Momma still considered him a pest and rarely missed an opportunity to say so.

As he spoke about how good Captain had treated him, my mind drifted off to the summer of 1958 when Ronnie came to us. He was a scared little boy whom I despised for no other reason than he followed me around like a lost puppy, but after awhile we got used to each other and by the end of summer we were friends. Then school started. Sara, the neighbor girl one year older than Ronnie, sat with him on the bus and introduced him to her friends. It didn't take him long to adjust to a new school and make friends. He was a nice kid and had a way about him that drew others in like a magnet draws in nails. By the time I graduated he was the most popular boy in his class and confessed to me he was glad his "real" mother and my Daddy never came back for him. After earning a degree in education at Ferris State University in Big Rapids below the Mackinac Bridge, he moved back to Brimley, married Sara, and was hired at Lake Superior State College. It won't surprise me if one day they make him president. I have no doubt that when he retires, he'll be given a seat on the Board.

He and Sara have one child and are expecting another in a few months. Ronnie insisted his first born be christened Olivia. He promised Sara she could name the next baby whatever she wanted. If the infant was a boy, he preferred Oliver. If another girl, he preferred Olive, but he reassured Sara the choice of a name was hers and hers alone. She rolls her eyes and smiles every time he makes these remarks. I think they're happy. Sara's father, Mr. Odell, built them a cottage next to the big house where he lives with his wife. He finally convinced Mrs. Odell that the Nazis were not coming to Michigan, but the way things are going, we can't be too sure. Ronnie's cough brings me back to the church and his eulogy.

"...took me in and treated me as his own son. Even asked if I would call him 'Dad' which I was proud to do. He taught me to drive and when I wrecked his car, he hugged me and said cars could be replaced, I couldn't." After a ten-minute monologue, Ronnie's face was wet with tears. Momma was horrified. She held up her hand and motioned him back to his pew. He thanked everyone for coming and finally stepped away from the altar. As he passed Momma, he patted her shoulder. At least I think it was a pat, but it might have been a pinch considering the slight squeal she emitted. Father Munch finished saying the requiem mass. When it was over, we followed the hearse to Oakland Chapel Gardens on M-129 where a few more words were said and a handful of dirt was tossed on Captain's coffin. Then we got back in our cars and drove to the church hall where the ladies had prepared a nice luncheon complete with pink petit fours ordered from the local bakery.

Everything looked perfect, and it was until Momma spied a fly swimming in the imitation cut-glass punch bowl. She had taken off her black hat with the dotted black veil so everyone could clearly see the look of horror on her face when she screamed. Father Munch was by her side and caught her before she collapsed on the new ceramic tile floor that Captain had paid for three months before his heart unexpectedly gave out. Ronnie and Sara rushed to Momma's side, but I held back. As much as I loved my mother, I wasn't fooled by her various ways of attracting attention.

While Momma was being fanned by Mrs. Odell and Father Munch was blessing her with cold Holy Water, I looked around the room. Unlike the dark, dreary church with its hard mahogany pews and Stations of the Cross nailed on the wall every few feet as a reminder of what Jesus did for us, the hall was bright and cheerful. After Sam Odell married Flint's sister, Jill, he settled down and joined Mr. Odell in his carpentry business. Sam did most of the painting and was good at it. I had long ago forgiven him for getting fresh with me when he was sixteen and I was twelve. By the time I was thirteen, I realized what a silly girl I had been to get scared when he pecked my cheek. He was taking some of the sideroad kids to the drive-in to see "Frankenstein." I was so frightened I demanded that he take me home two minutes after he had picked me up. Whenever the old gang gets together, we laugh at our youthful innocence.

"Do you think you've recovered enough to walk to the chair over there?" I heard Father Munch ask Momma as he pointed to a lovely old Queen Anne wing chair covered with expensive chintz fabric Captain had paid for last year after Momma complained the chair was too ugly for words. "I can bring it to you if you're still feeling faint," the priest said. His concern over my mother's strength was laughable. She was stronger than a rodeo bull, but she craved attention. It took me years to notice that the topic of any conversation we ever had always turned to her. Even when I tried to tell her she had hurt my feelings or practiced her passive-aggressive behavior towards me, it was she who ended up crying and I ended up apologizing.

It's a shame we can't pick our mothers. Most of my friends feel as I do. We get along great with our dads because we rarely see them or they just hand us money and tell us to scram, but our mothers are an entirely different breed. Throughout my youth and teenage years, I wished I could have waved a wand and made Momma disappear. Perhaps she didn't mean to be uppity, but that's the way she came across to the mothers of my friends. I was just like her until the sideroad kids set me straight. Without caring if I'd be drawing attention to myself and embarrassing Momma, I picked up a metal folding chair and walked out of the hall. The intense heat of the day was wearing off as a breeze blew from the north and cooled the afternoon. I placed the chair near a maple tree and my thoughts turned to a cold winter day just after Christmas many years ago.

It was a Saturday and I was exercising my horse, Sunflower. We were walking down the road when I saw my neighbor, Shirley Quails, heading in my direction. She waved. It would have been rude to pretend I hadn't seen her so I waved back. Then I cued Sunflower to turn back and gently kicked her, but instead of turning around, she trotted towards Shirley. She paid no attention to my commands and didn't stop until she was a nose away from her. When I saw what Shirley was wearing, I was horrified. Her plaid jacket belonged in the rag bag. It was ripped and torn. Her brown snowpants were patched at the knees and raveled around the ankles. Instead of a warm *chapeau* on her head, she was wearing an old bandana tied underneath her chin. I'm sure her grandmother had knit her scarf from leftover yarn because it was at least a hundred different colors. Her mittens were caked with snow that had hardened and turned into little dangling balls, but the most terrifying sight of all was her ice skates.

Instead of beautiful white figure skates like the new pair underneath my Christmas tree, she was wearing ugly old black ones. They must have belonged to a man because not even Shirley could have had feet that long. I almost felt sorry for her. I was wearing my new pink hat and snowsuit trimmed in pink rabbit fur. My matching leather gloves and riding boots were lined with real fur, although I didn't know what kind because I didn't know which animal gave its life so my hands and feet would be warm.

As I looked down at Shirley, I realized how awful it must be to be poor. My skates were still in the box. Momma said my skating lessons would begin as soon as she found a teacher who was good enough to work with me and show me how to spin and jump and perhaps even do a single axle. I said hello to Shirley and asked why she was skating on the road. She said there was no place else to skate. I thought that was a ridiculous answer because her father owned acres and acres of land. I asked why he didn't make a rink for her and Squeaky, and she said it was impossible because the land belonged to the cows. When I said cows didn't own anything as far as I knew, she told me they certainly did. Even your front yard I remember asking her. She ignored me and skated farther down the road. Sunflower was getting bored standing still. She started bucking. I had a hard time keeping her from rearing. I passed Shirley and said *au revoir* in my finest French accent. Shirley followed alongside us. I was horrified that she might skate all the way to my house. Momma wanted me to be friends with her, but I just couldn't.

For one thing, she had a peculiar odor that was a cross between mothballs and her grandmother's liniment. She lived in an old house, and her grandmother slept on a cot in the kitchen. The first time I met Shirley, she took me upstairs to meet her dolls. I thought she was crazy when she called them her *children.* When school started, I didn't want her to sit with me on the bus. I always looked out the window and pretended I didn't see her as she walked down the aisle. I would have died if she had sat next to me. She ignored me and always chose the seat behind me. I thought that was her way of tormenting me because I wouldn't be her friend even though we were in the same grade. In class she sat behind me, and I had to inhale her *odeur* all day. At that time, Momma was teaching me French. *La mauvaise odeur* are the polite words for an unpleasant smell. I didn't know the French word for stink and Momma was trying her best to raise me to be a lady so even if I had known the translation for stink, I wouldn't have said it. The road got icier the closer we got to my house. Shirley had skated ahead and was waiting by the garage. I was afraid Sunflower might slip and fall so I dismounted and led her by the reins. Shirley skated over to us and offered to take one of them. I told her I didn't need any help. I was miffed that this imbecile thought I was incapable of leading my own horse.

I was about to say so when I slipped and fell backwards. I dropped the reins, and Sunflower left the road and ran through the field towards the barn. I yelled at her, but she wouldn't come back. I was angry and my head hurt. I started crying. I thought Shirley would laugh at me like my Mackinac Island friends used to when I fell, but she didn't. She held out her hands and told me to grab hold so she could pull me up. I remember looking at her mittens with the dingle balls dangling from them. I didn't want to touch them. I thought their *odeur* would cling to my lovely new gloves so I told her I didn't need her help and could get up by myself. When I tried, I slipped again. Riding boots were made for stirrups not for icy country roads. I didn't know what to do. I cried until tears rolled down my cheeks. Shirley stared at me but didn't say anything. Then she pulled off her mittens and stuffed them in her jacket pockets. She knew I didn't want to touch them. I reached for her hands. I felt a little ashamed and asked why she hadn't laughed when I fell. She said it was rude to laugh at people. When we reached my driveway, the snow was too deep for her skates. She let go of my hand, turned around, put on her mittens, and skated home.

I remember feeling sad that she hadn't turned around and waved. For the first time since we had moved from the Island, I wanted a friend who didn't laugh when I fell or said something stupid. I wanted Shirley even though she was poor. I stood by the garage and watched her skate away until Momma opened the front door and told me to get in the house before I froze to death. She helped me take off my boots and snowsuit. Then she poured hot cocoa into my favorite cup, and we sat at the dining room table. I told her what had happened and that I was going to ask Captain to build a skating rink and invite Shirley and all the sideroad kids to use it. I said I didn't need professional lessons. The kids could help me.

"You look deep in thought," Flint said as he walked up to me. "You're gonna miss Captain, right? I know I sure will. He was one of the good guys."

"Yes, but I wasn't thinking about him. I was remembering the first time I realized what a good person Shirley was. Too bad she couldn't make it to the funeral. I haven't heard from her in months. Have you?"

"No, not lately. What are your plans, Liz, now that the lawsuit's over and you avoided prison?" Flint crossed his long legs and put his arm around the back of my chair. I was shocked when he showed up in a real suit instead of some hippie outfit. When he returned from Viet Nam, he had changed so much I hardly recognized him. Once discharged, he grew his hair long and dressed in psychedelic clothes that gave me a headache. After my divorce from Danny we dated a few times, but there wasn't a spark so we called it quits and agreed to be friends instead of lovers. I was more shocked than he was. Flint had been sweet on me since high school, at least that's what I thought, but then there was Candy. He was weak-kneed over her.

"That bogus suit really knocked the stuffing out of me. I wish Sims had left everything he owned to his cat. Would have made the past couple years easy for me. Nobody knew he had kinfolk up west in the Keweenaw. He never spoke of them. Everyone thought he was a bachelor. He never mentioned his three witchy sisters. When someone from the Soo called them and said he had made me his heir, they descended like vultures. God, what a mess I landed in."

"Sims loved you like the daughter he never had. Put it out of your mind and move on. Hey, Squeaky, grab a chair and c'mon over here. Liz needs cheering up." Shirley's twin brother was carrying a plate of food in one hand and a glass of punch in the other. He handed the food to Flint and reached for a silver flask in his pocket. After adding a splash of whiskey to the punch, he offered us a drink. Flint refused, but I grabbed and gulped. The booze felt good as it burned my throat.

"Hey, Liz, take it easy," Squeaky said. "Don't get plastered or your ma will have a fit. She sure looks swell in her short black dress and that crazy hat. Did she buy it or did she rob the feathers from one of Sam's chickens?" He laughed as I handed him the flask, a souvenir Blew had sent from Da Nang. Squeaky was lucky. He spent his time stateside and the only place he saw the war was on television. "There's nothing like a good meal after a funeral," he said. "The old gals sure know their way around a kitchen. Look at these biscuits. They're light as air."

"You guys have room for one more?" Fenders asked.

"We sure do," Flint said. "Captain would be mighty proud of you and your brood. By the way, where's Delores and the kids?"

"She stayed home. The heat's getting to her. She was at the wake last night and said that was enough. She didn't know Captain except as a customer, and a good one at that." Fenders hugged me. "Sure am sorry, Liz," he said. "At least he didn't suffer."

"Thanks, Fenders. That's what everybody says. I hope he didn't. He was a great stepdad to me."

"You kids got room for an old man?" Katie's grandpa asked. He rolled his wheelchair over to where we were. Flint jumped up and pushed the chair a little closer. "That's good enough, young man," he said. "This is like old times with everybody together and getting along." He wiped his eyes with a blue hanky he pulled from his pocket. "Well, it ain't quite like old times, not without Blew and Johnny." He shook his head and brushed strands of white hair from his forehead. He's at least eighty but doesn't look it. We all thought he'd die years ago when Jewel Red Nails passed away shortly before their wedding, but he didn't. Katie helped him get through his loss. Then when Johnny hung himself, we thought for sure his heart would give out, but it didn't. Even when Blew died, his ticker never stopped. "Has anyone seen Katie?" he asked. "Did she go off with that tall boy she brought home? He seems mighty sweet on her. Say, how about one of you getting me a cup of coffee with plenty of cream and sugar. Anybody got a hat I can borrow? The sun's in my eyes."

"I'll get your coffee," Fenders said. "And I've got a straw hat in my car. I'll get it for you."

"That'll be fine. Thank you, son."

"Grandpa, will you tell us a story like you did when we were young?" I asked. He always told the best tales. We'd gather around him and listen, but he never finished any of his stories, most likely because he couldn't think of a good ending. Ronnie loved listening to them. I guess we all did. I'm not going to have children. I decided that long before I married Danny, but I didn't tell him. That was one reason we divorced. He wanted a houseful of brats, but I said a couple cats were enough for me. It didn't take long to part after he learned the truth. Fenders returned with the coffee and the hat.

"Are you kids sure you want to hear a story?" Grandpa asked. "Are you sure you're not just being polite?" He sipped his drink and adjusted the hat so the sun wasn't in his eyes. Anyone could tell by looking at him he was anxious to talk. Captain had visited him almost every day last winter. Momma was mad because he was always a bit tipsy when he came home, but Captain said Grandpa liked his company and he liked Grandpa's Irish whiskey. Katie joined us. She looked beautiful. Her brown hair had golden highlights in it, and her yellow dress showed off her tan. She was tall and thin, but not skinny like that freaky English girl, Twiggy. Katie had always been pretty, but her outspoken ways and insistence on being the most intelligent person in class made her a target for girls who were jealous of her and envied the ease with which she glided from one boy to another. Her "tall" fellow wasn't with her.

"Katie," Grandpa said. "You're just in time for a story. Sit on that bench and I'll begin." In a minute Candy, Daisy, and Ronnie joined us. When Grandpa started talking, I think we all felt the same. For the first time in years, the sideroad kids were together, older and maybe even a little sadder, but together like we had been during the summers of our youth. Grandpa cleared his throat like he used to. We leaned towards him as if we were children.

"Did I ever tell you kids about our pet goat, Billy?" he asked. We reassured him he hadn't which wasn't true, but nobody cared. I felt tears sting my eyes and a lump come to my throat as I looked at my friends. Where had the years gone? Were Johnny and Blew listening to us from somewhere in heaven or were they floating around us? Was Jewel Red Nails with them? What about Mr. Sims? Was he with the others who had gone before us and waited while we lived out the days we were given? And where was Captain? Was he toasting Grandpa's health? We heard laughter coming from the hall. I was glad. Grandpa began his tale.

"Most of you remember Granny, my wife of many years before she decided to leave me one October morning and fly off to heaven, but what you don't know is how much she loved goats. Before Katie's mother came along, we lived in an old farmhouse that belonged to one of her kinfolk. It was a tumbledown shack that nobody wanted so it was give to us. There's always plenty of work to do around a place that's almost falling down and has a leaky roof and a barn that needs patching and a vegetable garden to put in and hay to be taken off before the rain ruins it. You kids know what it's like living on a farm. Why, the work's never done, especially in an old place. Just ask any farmer and he'll tell you that every word I'm telling you is the gospel truth especially in the summer when you can hear the grass growin' with every drop of rain and when lightning misses your house but hits your best maple tree and it's got to be…"

"Grandpa, will you please get on with your story?" Ronnie asked just as he had when he was six. Everyone laughed, especially Grandpa. "I want to hear the story before Sara has our baby."

"Hold your horses, young feller," Grandpa said. That had always been one of his favorite sayings. "Didn't I tell you kids years ago that a good story was like good wine? It needed time to mature." We agreed so he hooked his thumbs behind his suspenders and continued. "It was like this. I'd done the morning chores and had come in the kitchen and sat on my chair and closed my eyes for a little snooze when all of a sudden I heard Granny yelling like there was no tomorrow. I shook myself awake and headed for the front porch that was much like the one we used to gather around when you kids were kids and…" Everyone groaned, thinking he was getting off track and would start talking about the old days unrelated to his story as he had always done, but he fooled us.

"…and that's when I saw Hank Snippet's truck backing over our garden. Snippet was from Stalwart. He raised goats and be danged if he hadn't brought one with him that had a rope around its neck. I started yelling at him to git off the garden as Granny ran to get the goat Snippet was lifting from the bed of his truck. She didn't care two hoots about the garden. Snippet handed her the rope with the goat, and she handed him something that looked like a wad of bills. He jumped back in his truck and took off before I had time to get down the steps. I asked Granny what was going on. 'I bought a goat,' she said. 'His name is Billy. Now you'll never have to cut the grass because Billy will do it for us.'" Grandpa stopped talking and asked if anyone had something to put in his coffee that was stronger than cream. Squeaky pulled out his flask. Grandpa laughed, thanked him, and continued.

"Granny said Billy was six months old. She said he had a gentle and affectionate nature. She said if the nanny that birthed him hadn't strayed from her pen, he'd be a full-blooded Angora, but as it was, he was a cinnamon-colored mongrel that suited her just fine. She said he didn't need papers to prove his worth. I wasn't sure how I felt about having a young kid around the place. They're like undisciplined children. They get into everything that's none of their business, but as I watched Granny stroke his coat, I knew I was licked. I couldn't deprive her of something she loved. You kids know what that's like. You love your kids, but I'm sure sometimes you wish they'd disappear—go to their grandmother's or a friend's house or anywhere just to get them out of your hair." He wiped his forehead with his hanky. He looked tired. I was sure he wouldn't finish this story anymore than he had ever finished one when we were kids, but I was wrong.

"Jewel stopped by later that morning. She knew about the goat deal and wanted to see what he looked like. I was in an outbuilding fixing my arch nemesis—Pa's old red tractor with the steel wheels—and told Jewel Granny was somewhere outside. Jewel found her in the garden where Billy was nibbling leaf lettuce and the tops of carrots and beets. I knew he'd eat the entire garden if we didn't stop him, but Granny didn't seem to mind. It took some talking, but I finally convinced her to let me put a stake in the ground and the rope around it so Billy could eat as much grass as he wanted. She agreed but only after I found a much longer rope that gave him plenty of room to roam. Did I ever tell you kids about the barn my Pa built? Why, it was the best barn in the county. It was…"

"Grandpa, finish your story," Katie said. "What happened to Billy? People are starting to leave, and we're ready to go, too. Is there a point you're trying to make?"

"Your Grandmother loved that goat, Katie. When your mother was three or four, Granny taught her how to hitch Billy to a cart. One year they led the Fourth of July parade down Ashmun Street in the Soo. Through kindness and good care, Billy lived a long and happy life." Grandpa stopped talking and looked at the faces of the adults surrounding him. I was sure he saw us as the children he had known. Maybe he grieved for our future.

"My story is over, kids," he said. "I think Captain had a send-off he'd be proud of. He was a good man, and I'm going to miss him." Grandpa took off his glasses and wiped his face. He looked old and tired. Katie put her arms around him and soon we all did. We knew what he was thinking. That this story might be the last he would ever tell us as we went our separate ways. Fenders would go home and help Delores run the store. Flint would be busy working on his farm in Rudyard and taking care of his elderly uncle. Squeaky and Rachel were living on the farm and raising their twins. When summer was over, Daisy would return to Dublin and her career as an English Lit teacher. We didn't know if Candy would stay in the Upper Peninsula or return to Mississippi and try to patch things up with her husband. Ronnie and Sara were anxious to get going and finish packing. They were leaving in the morning for the Dells in Wisconsin for a week's vacation. I was ready to take Momma home where she could finally collapse on her chaise lounge, light a cigarette, and drink half a bottle of Hennessy. Grandpa asked if someone would wheel him back to the hall. He, too, was ready to go. I thanked him for coming to Captain's funeral. Grandpa said he wouldn't have missed it for the world.

The sunset was beautiful that evening. I sat on the porch swing and watched the day disappear. I knew things would be different now that Captain was gone. His lawyer would read his will in a few days. I didn't know what was in it, but it didn't matter. Everything I needed he had given me during his lifetime. Most important was learning to accept people as they are. That was the greatest gift of all.

Johnny

I'm standing in line with the rest of my classmates waiting to walk into the school gym for Baccalaureate Sunday. Once we get through this, there's only class night on Tuesday and graduation Thursday night and then it's all over. No more homework or teachers yelling at us. No more kidding around with my buddies—Blew, Flint, and Squeaky. No more carrying Katie's books from one class to the next. I'll miss that more than anything.

The place is packed and there's no air conditioning. I feel sweat trickling down my armpits. I hoped Ma would be among the parents, maybe even sitting next to Pa, but I scanned the audience and she's not here. My heart feels like lead. I haven't seen her since I was in sixth grade. I'll never know what I did to make her run away with the preacher from Kinross and never come back.

Mr. Keller walks by and thumps my shoulder. "Well, Johnny," he said. "It's all over but the crying. Bet you're going to miss Brimley High. Got any plans for college?" Mr. Keller's been our music teacher for as long as I can remember. Nobody knows if he has any idea how to play an instrument other than the piano. Blew figured he was the best our school could afford so they didn't make him audition before they gave him the job. He's a funny old guy. He wears the same brown suit every day. His pants are so shiny, Flint bet me a ten spot that before baccalaureate is over, Mr. Keller will slide out of his chair if the preachers are long-winded. I didn't bother to take him up on it. I'd have lost the bet for sure. What hair he has left is mostly gray. The dentist made him a lower plate, but his top teeth must be good because he still has one gold front tooth.

"No plans yet, Sir," I said. I wish he'd move on.

"Have you registered for the draft? You know there's going to be war. If Johnson and Westmorland keep sending men to Viet Nam, it won't be long before young fellows like you will be called to defend our country against communism. It's the domino effect, you know. The domino effect. Which branch do you prefer?" As he talks, he chews Blackjack gum and smokes a cigar. He blows smoke in my face. It's so thick it looks like he's drawn a gray veil between us.

His talk about war makes me more nervous. I feel sweat beginning to roll down my back. Mr. Keller coughs, and the wad of gum leaves his mouth and lands on my shoe. His gold tooth looks like it wants to follow it. He doesn't seem to notice he lost his gum or that his tooth is loose. "The Army, same as most of the other guys," I said. Now my palms are sweating. I wish I'd stayed home. I wanted to but Pa said it was important to take part in all the graduation traditions and spend time with my classmates. I don't know why. Other than the sideroad kids, I don't have any friends. Kids who live in Brimley thought I wasn't worth the effort because Pa owns a pig farm.

"If you're chicken, you can always make a run for the Yukon Territory," Mr. Keller was saying. "Uncle Sam would never find you in the Canadian wilderness." He laughs, pounds my back again, and moves on to the next kid. I feel sick. I wish I hadn't eaten all that bacon for breakfast. The grease is sitting heavy in my gut. I wish Katie was close to me. She'd settle my nerves like she always does. I don't know what I'd do without her. She wouldn't wear my class ring when we ordered them last year, but she didn't accept one from any other guy either. I'm going to propose after the graduation party her mother's throwing for us. I'll wait until everyone's gone and we're sitting on her porch swing. She might hesitate and make some excuse about going to college before getting engaged, but I expect that. I'll wait as long as it takes for her to be my wife.

The band's starting to warm up. It won't be long before we leave the hallway and march into the gym. Pa spent a fortune on my new clothes. I told him not to bother because I'll be wearing a gown like everyone else. Nobody in the audience will see anything except the cuffs of my pants and my shoes. Besides, nobody notices a guy's clothes. It would be different if Ma was here. I'd want to look good for her. Katie doesn't care what I look like. I know I'm not handsome like Flint or Danny, but Katie says there's a lot more to a person than just looks. My front teeth cross and I have freckles. Ma once said they'd fade when I was older, but I'm eighteen and the only thing that faded is Ma. Katie said she likes my teeth because they're different, but she's never said she likes the freckles.

I've loved her since we were toddlers and rode our tricycles on the road. We didn't live far apart. One day Ma told me to scram so I got on my trike and scrammed down the road until I came to the first lane. I turned down it and met a little girl heading towards me going at top speed. Her head was down and her brown braids were tied at the end with blue ribbons that looked like they were flying. She was wearing a blue shirt, blue shorts, and blue shoes. If I hadn't turned my trike to the side, she would have plowed into me. I remember saying "whoa" as if she was a horse. That's when she stopped and looked at me. I could tell she'd been crying. Her face was wet, and tears were rolling down her cheeks. I thought she was the nicest thing I'd ever seen.

"I ain't no horse," she sobbed. "You could have beeped your horn." She wiped her eyes with the back of her hand. It was as tan as a hazelnut. "Git out of my way," she commanded, but I didn't move. I remember saying she couldn't tell me to 'git' because I wasn't a dog. That's when she started bawling like a calf weaned from its mother. She said a car had run over Sassy last night and the driver didn't stop and pick her up and knock on their door and say he was sorry for killing her.

That's when I got off my trike and walked over to her. I patted her little brown hand like I'd seen Pa do when Ma was sad. I mumbled something about Sassy being in doggy heaven. She screamed at me and said Sassy wasn't a dog. She was her best doll and there wasn't a heaven for toys, not even if one was a beautiful doll that had been a Christmas present from Santa. I didn't know what to say so I said nothing. I just stood next to her and continued patting her hand until she pulled it away and wiped her face.

"What's your name?" she asked.

"Johnny," I said. "What's yours?"

"Katie," she said and that's the day I lost my heart to Kathleen Marie Clark. We were three years old.

Blew taps my shoulder, jolting me back to the present. I turn and look at him. His face is beet red. "Boy, am I mad," he says. He's punching his fist into the palm of his left hand. He was steaming.

"What are you mad at?"

"Not what, who. Who do you think? Daisy, of course. That gal's gonna be the death of me."

"What'd you do now?" Blew and Daisy are always fighting. She's a perfectionist, and he's a slob. He tries to please her, but it's impossible. She's always complaining about something. Blew's anger will take my mind off what Mr. Keller asked me. If I don't get the answer I want from Katie, my future's going to be rough, and it won't be on account of the war. I won't give up, though. I'll take it slow. Convincing her she won't find a better fellow will be like breaking a wild horse. Slow and steady will win in the end. "Well, what'd you do this time to upset her?"

"I wore the wrong shoes. Do you believe it? She took one look at my brown pants and black loafers with the penny in them and threw a fit. I swear, Johnny, I'm gonna divorce that woman before I marry her. Why does she have to be so bossy? Katie ain't like that with you. She don't give a hoot what you wear or if your hair is brushed or if there's manure on your good shoes. Women." Blew grunts.

"I wouldn't call Daisy a woman. She's the youngest kid in our class. She won't be eighteen until July." Blew rolls his eyes.

"For cryin' out loud. You know what I mean. Don't act stupid. Crap, the gym got quiet. Must be time to march in. Let's get this show goin' so I can get my hotrod on the road." Blew continues grumbling under his breath. Mrs. Lark starts barking orders. She tells us to stand up straight and keep our arms at our sides with our hands in a fist and our thumbs over our fingers. She says we must not gawk around but keep our eyes glued to the head in front of us. You'd think we were soldiers. The band starts playing something that sounds like a hymn. We march in, find our seats, and sit down after the band plays our national anthem.

The preachers are on the stage. Principal Jackson introduces them as each one takes the podium, says a prayer, and blabs about the importance of making a positive contribution to society. There's a priest from the Catholic Church in Brimley, a preacher from the Congregational Church down the road from the school, and a couple other men in black. I don't know who they are, but I know one thing for sure. I don't like preachers. I'll never forgive the one who stole Ma.

I'm not interested in what they're saying because I know it's all lies. Preachers and priests are no better than anyone else. They just dress different. I look at the back of Katie's head. She's our valedictorian, but she won't give her speech today. She asked me to help her write it, but I couldn't be any help because I barely scraped by. If it wasn't for her, I might have flunked a couple grades. It's not that I'm stupid. It's just that I don't like book learning unless I'm learning about pigs. There's always something new, and pig farmers have to stay up on things or go under. That's what Pa tells me.

Katie likes to wrap her feet around the rungs of chairs. I look down and see she's kicked off her high heels. Her feet are long and slender. Her toes are fiddling with the rungs which is hard to do with nylons on, but Katie can do anything. She was homecoming queen and I was her escort. She was beautiful in a dark blue dress with a sash on her left shoulder. A diamond pin held the sash in place. The diamonds weren't real, but they sparkled when the light hit them. I was the proudest boy in the gym when we walked in. I held her hand and guided her up the steps to the stage. I knew she'd be voted queen. Everybody loves Katie.

As the preachers drone on, my mind wanders through the years we spent in school. Seventh grade was easier than I thought, but eighth was awful. It was the year Katie walked by me when she got on the bus instead of sitting with me as she usually did. She sat with Candy. They talked and giggled all the way to school and all the way home. I wondered why girls were so silly until I realized guys were the same except we didn't giggle. We whistled and told each other which gals were easy and which ones to steer clear of. Ninth grade was a blur, but tenth was the grade I'll never forget. It was the year I kissed her for the first time.

"...as you leave here today, remember what you have heard and be guided by the words of these holy men who are wiser than you can ever hope to be," Principal Jackson was saying. "Be humble in wherever the future has in store for you. Accept your fate without rancor." The band played another hymn. I watched the "holy men" walk off the stage and wondered if they were going home to their wives or meeting women from the Soo's red light district. I wondered if they were anxious to get their hands on their Bible or a bottle of gin in the glovebox of their cars. The bitterness I felt towards so-called men of the cloth made me sick. We left the gym, and I got in the car with Pa.

"You looked good," he said. "Your Ma would have been proud." I didn't bother to answer. Pa knew as well as I did that if she had cared for either of us, she'd never have left. I felt sorry for him. I think he still loves her. I might too, but I've tried to bury those feelings. I learned a long time ago that longing for her won't bring her back and will only make me sad. "Want to stop for an ice cream?" Pa asked.

"Sure," I said, but what I really wanted to do was open the car door and roll out. The sweat from my armpits wasn't the only place I felt wet. I kept wiping my forehead, and my back was soaked. It wasn't just the heat making me perspire. It was not knowing what answer Katie would give me on Thursday. If she refused me and rejected me after all my years of devotion, it'd be awful hard to take. "A triple chocolate cone sounds great, Pa. Thanks for asking."

"You're welcome, son. Horsefeather's is open. He's cheap on the scoops, but I don't feel like driving to the Soo."

"It's okay," I said. We're polite to each other like two strangers meeting for the first time. We've been like this since Ma left. Pa never yells at me or scolds me, and I never break the rules. I don't drink or smoke or chase girls like Flint does. I do my chores and help Pa with the pigs. I never complain about anything, not even when Coach Leo asked me to be on the basketball team and Pa said no. I wanted to play more than anything and I was good at it, but Pa said he couldn't be driving me to the home games and couldn't pick me up when we played Cedarville or Pickford or any other away game. And he wouldn't let me drive his truck. He said I might hit an icy spot and wreck it. I didn't argue. I nodded my head and went to my room that looked out on the fields. I put my fist through the wall and patched it the next day. If Pa knew, he never said anything. He pulled into Horsefeather's and we got out. I ordered my cone. Pa ordered a vanilla double dip. We walked down to the water and sat on a log.

Lake Superior waves rushed to the shore and back again. I watched the whitecaps as if they were fighting each other to be the first to touch the sand. I thought about all the times Sam Odell had driven the sideroad kids to the beach. The water was always cold, but we didn't care. We ran into Superior as if we were running towards something wild and wonderful. I wasn't a good swimmer, not like the others who had learned to swim in our river. If I stayed close to the riverbank, I wasn't afraid, but this lake terrified me. It was so vast. So strong. So eager to pull me under. We heard a blast and saw two freighters heading upbound. Their destination was probably Duluth.

"I always thought I'd like to be a sailor," Pa said. "But when my Pa died, I buried that dream and took over the farm. You didn't know that, did you? You didn't know I wanted to sail so bad it was like an ache that wouldn't go away. Did you ever wonder why I carve ships when the day's work is done?" I was about to answer but he continued talking. It was as if he had stored up a whole lot of words and wherever they were stored there were too many to stay put so they tumbled out. "Lake Superior beckoned me like a woman entices a man to follow her. I used to sneak out at night when there was a full moon and walk to Alcott Beach. I'd sit on a log much like this one and dream about being a sailor. I missed the war, you know. My brother took my place because one of us had to stay on the farm and care for Ma. He went down with his ship when they were crossing the Atlantic and were torpedoed by a German sub. He was a Navy man. Planned on making it his career. Died when he was only twenty-three." As if coming back from the past and his dream of sailing he asked, "How's your ice cream?"

"Good," I said. I didn't look at him. I knew he'd be embarrassed. He never mentions World War II. Most of his friends joined up when Pearl Harbor was bombed. Some came back to Brimley. Some were buried in France or the Philippines or Africa or wherever they died. I think he felt guilty that duty kept him home and out of harm's way. "You can't beat an ice cream cone on a hot day," I said. My words sounded hollow.

"About ready to go?" he asked. He got up and took a long look at the water, then turned and walked up the path to the car. I watched him. He was tall and thin, but strong. He walked erect. His black suit was old, but he'd taken it to Crisp's Laundry and had it cleaned and pressed. He'd spent an hour shining his shoes until he could almost see his face in them. I rarely looked at Pa's face. I knew the lines across his forehead had been etched there a long time ago, but I'd only recently noticed the deep lines running down his face and on both sides of his mouth. I don't know when his blue eyes turned green, but turned they had.

"Are you coming?" he called. He had started the car and stuck his head out the window. "It's past milking time. Poor old Bessie will be wondering where we are." In a second I was in the passenger's seat and we were heading home. We rode in silence, but Pa's words were swirling in my mind. I wondered what other dreams he had when he was young and how they had been thwarted. "War's coming," he said almost in a whisper. He kept looking straight ahead. "I love you, Johnny."

"You, too, Pa. I love you, too. Don't worry about Viet Nam. It won't get me."

"Maybe your number won't come up until it's over."

"Maybe," I said. We turned in the driveway, changed our clothes, and did the chores. I felt certain I wouldn't be drafted, at least not for a long time.

The next couple days went fast. Class night was over with silly predictions of what each of us would do as adults. Katie acted as a news commentator and mixed up the kids that were supposed to walk on the stage together. It was her way of embarrassing the snobs. It worked, too, except that she forgot Squeaky and Russell who were supposed to be future farmers. They were mad and told her so. She felt bad but said they should have yelled from the stage wings, "Hey, what about us?" but they didn't. They went home, but the rest of us went to Monocle Lake. We'd been there for only a couple minutes when kids grabbed Katie and threatened to throw her in the lake. She fought like a tiger—kept swinging her arms and hitting anyone within reach. She was screaming. Blew and I tried to help her, but we were jumped from behind. A couple older boys, who had a campfire farther down the beach, heard the commotion and came to her rescue. When Flint arrived in his jalopy and learned what had happened, he drove her home, and I went with them.

After we dropped her off, we went back and beat the daylights out of the kids who had tried to hurt her.

I awoke early this morning and was up before Pa. When he came downstairs, the coffee was perking, and I was frying bacon. "Sure smells good in here," he said. "I could get used to this." I asked how many eggs he wanted. He said three would be enough. I tossed them in the pan with the bacon grease. The pan was hot and the egg whites crisped around the edges just the way he liked them. I set his plate in front of him and poured coffee in his favorite cup—the one he wouldn't wash because he said the residue made the coffee taste better. "What a feast," he said. I fried two more eggs and filled my plate with bacon and toast. When Pa got up and walked to the stove to get more coffee, he patted my shoulder, something he hadn't done since I was nine years old and Ma was here.

"It's your last day of school," he said. "I'm proud of you. You'll be a big help to me on the farm if you stay. You do plan on staying after graduation?" he asked. He didn't take his eyes from the steam rising from his cup.

"Sure, I'm staying. You couldn't manage without me." I tried to sound cheerful, but my mind was whirling with plans that had nothing to do with raising pigs.

"You're a good boy. I'll do the chores this morning. It'll be the last time you'll be working for me. From tomorrow on, we'll be partners." He walked to the cupboard and took an envelope out of a drawer. "This makes it official," he said. "I had a lawyer draw it up." He handed me a deed with our names on it. "If she ever comes back, she won't have any claim on the property. You'll never have to worry about losing your home or the business." Before I could say anything, he was out the door. Bessie would be waiting near the barn for her first milking.

I could have wept. I'm like that fellow Fenders used to write home about. The guy's name was Kenny. He was always crying about something. It didn't matter if it was good or bad. Fenders said he was killed when a military dump truck ran over him. He said his last words were something about making sure his ma got money from the government. Fenders said he died in his arms before the medics got to him. Thinking about Kenny—a boy I'd never met—made me wonder if everything we do is predestined like some people believe. We learned about the Calvinists in school. I think there was one line in our history book about them. I wonder if Ma was predestined to leave when I was eleven. Maybe she wanted to return, maybe she even tried a few times, but that darn predestination held her back.

I poured water into the granite dishpan and put it on the woodstove. While I waited for it to heat, I wiped the table and swept the floor. I swatted a couple flies that had been walking around the rim of the butter dish. I filled the salt shaker. Then I shook the cigarette ashes out of Pa's ashtray. When the water was hot, I washed the dishes. I rinsed out Pa's cup, but I didn't put the dishrag in it. I dried everything and put the dishes and silverware back in the cupboard. There was one piece of bacon left in the cast iron pan. I opened the back door and called to Champ. He came running. He loved bacon better than anything. In dog years, he was forty-two, but he acted like a pup. He'd be good company for Pa if I wasn't here. When the kitchen was as neat as I could make it, I walked upstairs to my room.

I looked at the picture of Katie on my nightstand. It was taken two years ago. She was wearing a light blue sweater that buttoned. The top two buttons were undone. Her brown hair was short. She wasn't wearing her glasses. Her eyelashes were long. Her dimples were almost as deep as Sam's. Her smile was natural. It didn't look forced like some of the smiles of our classmates. Every night I kissed her lips. She never felt my kiss through the glass, but she felt it the night of the mixer after our last basketball game. We were in the tenth grade, and it was the first time I'd had the nerve to kiss her. She didn't seem to mind. It only lasted a second, maybe even less, maybe no time at all, but it was pure heaven to me. It was the last dance of the night. Gene Pitney's "Town Without Pity" was playing, and I finally did what I had been dreaming about since I was three years old.

I took my good suit out of the closet and picked a strand of Katie's hair from the lapel. She hugged me Sunday before we put on our caps and gowns. I taped the strand to the back of the picture frame. Might seem like a stupid thing to do, but nobody will ever see it. Graduation won't be until eight o'clock tonight, but I want to make sure my clothes are ready. Last night I ironed the dark blue slacks Katie likes, and I polished my loafers. I put a shiny new penny in both of them. I got my hair cut last week so it looks good. The whitewalls behind my ears aren't too noticeable. I don't have any pimples, and the scar on my forehead doesn't look bad. Unlike my freckles, it faded over the years. We don't have a full-length mirror, but from what I can see in the bathroom mirror, I look okay. I'm ready for the day and whatever it brings.

I made my bed and put the screen in the window. I like the way my curtains billow out when the breeze blows through them. Ma made them. She loved to sew and was always cutting out new fabric she laid across the kitchen table after she cleaned it good so no grease would spoil the cloth. The old curtains in my room were plastic. She hated them. They came with the house Pa bought after his mother died, and he sold the farm where he'd grown up. He wasn't married at the time. Plastic curtains didn't bother him. The window shades were dark green. Ma hated those, too, and took them down, but she didn't throw them away. One day I found them hidden behind the stairs and put them back where they belonged. During the summer, they keep the sun out of my room so it doesn't get too hot. If Ma was angry, she didn't let on, and the shades stayed.

I look around my room. It's sparse, but good enough for me. There's my bed and nightstand holding Katie's picture and a brown clock radio. For years I kept a photo of Ma on it, but when I gave up hoping she'd come back, I put it in a drawer of the nightstand. An old chair in the corner is where I throw my clothes that need washing. Once a month Pa takes a load to the laundromat in the Soo. We don't use the wringer washer. That's another thing Ma hated. She wanted a real washer and dryer, but Pa said they were too expensive, and he'd buy them when the pig farm started making money. We're in the chips now, but he says it's best to be careful about spending money because nobody can predict the future.

I leave my bedroom door open, run down the stairs, and grab some lumps of sugar from the bowl on the table. Then I head out to the pasture where Butterball's waiting for her morning treat. She's a good old girl and nuzzles my hand as she looks for more. It's a beautiful May morning with a clear sky. I notice things like that because a farmer has to know the weather. It doesn't affect us as much as it would if we raised cattle and had to take off hay. With only one milk cow, Pa makes a deal with Blew's grandfather. He gives us hay and we give him enough pork to last the winter. No money exchanges hands. I think bartering's a great way to live. Nobody's out anything, and farmers don't have to spend money they don't have. Ma hated the system.

It's almost time for the bus to come. I give Butterball one last pat and head for the shed where Pa's sorting through old boards for another pigpen he's going to build. "Bye," I say. His back is to me, and I must have startled him. His shoulders jerked. "Sorry, Pa. I didn't mean to scare you."

"You caught me deep in thought, that's all," he said.

"Have you found the boards you wanted?"

"No, but that's not what I was thinking about. I was remembering the day I made your cradle. Some of the wood I used is still here. It brings back memories. Have a good day, Johnny." He shook my hand. I thanked him and walked to the road. The bus rounded the corner and screeched to a halt. I got on and took the same seat I'd taken since kindergarten. Katie's stop was next. She sat with me.

The day went much as I thought it would. Blew and Flint cracked up some of the teachers. They were always the class clowns. Danny told everybody he'd been accepted at Michigan Tech in Houghton to study some kind of engineering. Daisy said she was going to spend the summer in Detroit with her aunt and uncle. Everybody groaned. We thought she was crazy to leave the sideroad and go to a hot city, but she insisted it was important to see the Detroit Institute of Arts, the GM building, Belle Isle, and lots of other places we'd never heard of. Blew and Russell reported that until their draft notices arrived, they'd be laborers at construction sites whenever Sam's dad needed them. Flint said he'd be helping his uncle run his farm in Rudyard. And so it went. The kids told the teachers what they'd be doing and where they'd be going. When asked, I said I'd be staying home working with Pa until Uncle Sam called me. Before we knew it, the last bell rang for the last time. We piled in the busses and went home.

At the graduation ceremony a few hours later, Katie's valedictorian address was great and so was the party her mother gave us. There was only one snag to a day that had started out so good, so full of promise. After the party when everyone was gone, I asked Katie to marry me. She was quiet for a long time before she took my hand and said she loved me but there was so much she wanted to do before getting married that she couldn't promise me anything. I asked her to wear my class ring, but she refused. She said it wouldn't be right. She was leaving tomorrow to work in a fudge shop on Mackinac Island. She said she'd be gone all summer. In the fall, she was going to be a freshman at Michigan State University. She said she wouldn't see me again for three months and it would only be for a few hours because there was so much to do before her parents drove her to East Lansing. After that, she wouldn't be home until Christmas. Then she kissed my cheek and said it was time for me to go. It had been a long day, and she was tired.

I walked down the road like a zombie. I felt numb. The moon was bright, and the sky was full of stars. It was a beautiful night. Somewhere in the distance, an owl hooted three times. A dog barked. A horse whinnied. It was late, about eleven o'clock. Pa always went to bed early, but tonight he had stayed up. I could see him sitting in his chair by the open window. I knew he was waiting for me. I was walking towards the house when I suddenly felt a strange urge. I turned towards the barn and climbed the ladder to the haymow. That's when I tripped over the rope I had put there a week ago.

I saw Ma's face flash before me. In that moment, I knew she was dead. It all became clear why she had never returned. Whether the preacher had killed her or whether she had died from cancer or some other disease, I'd never know. What I did next was due to a strange and powerful force that had taken hold of me. It must have been predestined from my birth or maybe it was some odd domino effect, but it didn't matter what it was that made me reach for the rope. I slung it over a rafter, climbed on the bales and secured it. I made a noose, but it felt like someone from another dimension, another planet was tightening the knots. As I slipped it around my neck, I heard Pa calling my name. I heard Butterball neighing, but it was too late. I had become one with the moon and the stars. At last

I had found Ma. I saw my arms reach for her, but she turned her back on me and disappeared and then I was gone.

Blew

"C'mon boys, let's get this over with," I said. "If we hang around Lazy Bob's much longer, we might change our minds and head for Canada and forget all about where we're supposed to be goin' tomorrow." Flint and Russell are sitting on either side of me at Lazy Bob's in Brimley. We're trying to get drunk, but the bartender won't let us. We were hoping the Army had forgotten all about Upper Peninsula boys, but no dice. Our draft notices came through so our good time's over.

"Just one more," Flint said as he emptied his glass, but Bob said we'd had enough. There was a serious look on his face. He knows about war. He's been in one, and a piece of shrapnel stayed in his thigh as a souvenir of his time when the Normandy beaches were stormed. He extended his hand to each of us.

"God be with you, fellows. You're going to need divine protection if you're sent overseas. That's what saved me."

"Thanks, Bob," Flint said. "Don't worry about these two. They're tough as nails. If they have to, they'll show the Viet Cong who's boss. I'll be joining them in a month. I can't wait. The three of us will put the Cong on the run." I turned my stool to the right and glanced at Flint. His eyes betrayed his feelings. He didn't look as brave as he sounded. Bob didn't say anything.

I looked around the bar. I wanted to remember every detail. It was what Daisy would call beautiful. The mahogany in front of us was thick as a tree trunk and worn smooth as glass from years of men leaning on it. When sunlight hit the bottles behind the bar, their contents took on the color of the glass. Hennessy and Old Crow were golden. Crème de menthe looked like emeralds. The mirror behind the booze reflected our faces. We didn't look very happy. I turned away and downed the last of my beer. "Drink up, guys. Time to go. See you, Bob." He came around from the bar, opened the door, and saluted us. "Stay safe," he said. We piled into the Pontiac Grandpa Marvin had given me on my sixteenth birthday. I honked the horn as we drove away.

"Hey, Blew, watch where you're going," Flint yelled. "You almost hit the bridge. What're you trying to do? Knock us off before the Cong does?" He laughed. Flint's a good guy. He never complains, but I wonder what he'll say when it's his turn and they cut off his long hair and shave his sideburns. Maybe he'll man up like Elvis. The King didn't cry when he sat in the barber's chair. He kept smiling and singing. I'd give anything to meet him one day and let him know Mam named me after him. 'Course I wouldn't say Elvis is my third name. Might make him feel third best.

I dropped Flint off at his place. Russell's spending the night with me. My grandparents will drive us to the Soo in the morning. We'll catch the Greyhound heading for Detroit. Earlier this evening, when we were at the supper table, everybody was quiet. Mam had made my favorite meal—pork chops, mashed potatoes, gravy, creamed peas and carrots, biscuits, and apple pie loaded with vanilla ice cream. It was a feast. For the first time since he was a pup, Utah didn't beg for a piece of whatever was on my plate. He rested his head on my lap. He's an old dog and knew something was going on. He watched every move I made as I packed my suitcase, and he whimpered when he heard Mam cry. I hope he don't die while I'm gone.

Just before dark Russell called his parents. His pa's sick and his ma can't leave him. That's why they won't see him off tomorrow. I couldn't hear what he was saying, but when he joined us on the porch, I knew he'd been cryin'. It's tough on all of us. We don't want to go, but Uncle Sam said we have to or spend a couple years in the slammer. No man worth his salt would choose that. And we're not cowards. We might not be brave, but we sure ain't yellow-bellied. I watched as dew covered the land I've known all my life. I never paid any attention to it before, but now I know why Daisy says the Upper Peninsula is God's gateway to heaven. Our porch faces west. I watched the sun fill the sky with colors I can't describe, and I can hardly believe that same sun is shining on soldiers in Viet Nam as they kill each other. Everything is peaceful. I don't imagine the battlefields know such peace. Utah's by my side.

Perkins, our cat, is curled in a ball on my lap. Russell's leaning against the screen door. Mam's rocking chair squeaks as she moves back and forth. Grandpa's sitting next to me, his unopened Bible on his lap.

"Blew," he said. "You've been a good boy." He took off his glasses and wiped his eyes with a bandana. He reached for the snuff box in his shirt pocket and put a pinch of Copenhagen behind his lower lip. He started to open the Bible but changed his mind. He put it on the bench behind him. I couldn't bring to mind when he hadn't read some verses from it. He used to pray all the time. When my draft notice arrived, it was like he lost belief in what he had always believed in. I felt sorry for him. All my life I heard him quote from that Bible and now it seems to mean nothing to him. Part of me is glad, but the other part of me—the part that's facing the unknown—hopes he starts praying again because we want to make it home alive and in one piece. God might listen to Grandpa's prayers because he sure didn't listen to mine when I prayed I wouldn't get drafted.

The sun sunk behind the barn and the woods behind it, and nobody said anything. Russell continued humming. I didn't know the tune, but Mam did. It was a hymn. She sang so soft I couldn't hear the words. We stayed on the porch until the sun disappeared completely, leaving only streaks of orange and red above the horizon. Nobody wanted to go in the house even though the mosquitoes were getting thick. Finally, Grandpa said it was time for Russell and me to hit the hay. We said goodnight. My grandparents hugged me and shook Russell's hand. They closed the kitchen door but didn't come upstairs. I heard Mam crying when she thought we were out of earshot. The noise she made was awful. It sounded like she was choking. I motioned Russell to go on. I hung back and listened.

"We should have told him years ago," Mam said when she could talk without sobbing. "Why did we keep it a secret from him?"

"It was the right thing to do at the time," Grandpa said. "He can't miss what he's never had. It's all in the past. Hush, now. The boys will hear you."

As I stood outside the kitchen door, I wondered if I should open it and tell them I knew what they were talking about—that both my parents were dead. I also knew when and how they died. My Ma died giving me birth, and my Pa shot himself. I was twelve the summer Flint discovered the letter his Uncle Leo wrote explaining everything. Flint gave me the letter, and I hid it in the bottom of a steamer trunk in the attic. No one will ever find it, at least I don't think so. I heard the snap of the kitchen light and didn't want my grandparents to find me listening so I ran up the stairs.

There were two metal beds in my room. Russell had taken the smaller one. Mam called it a three-quarter bed and had kept the original sheets that by now were threadbare. Russell and I said goodnight. He fell asleep fast. His breathing sounded normal, but I couldn't sleep. When I closed my eyes, I saw Daisy. She cried today. She tried to blink back the tears, but when I put my arms around her, it was like a dam broke. She poured her heart out as her tears flooded my shirt. She promised she'd write every day and tell me all the news. I fought back my own tears. I'm a man now, and men heading to war don't cry. We're brave. We have to be. We can't break down like women do because if we did, it would be worse for them. It don't matter how we feel inside. We gotta hide our feelings and be strong. We put on a good front, but if truth be told, we're just as scared as little kids getting on the school bus for the first time.

Moonlight streamed through my open window reminding me of the old days. Childhood seemed so long ago. I wondered if other guys were thinking the same thing as they spent their last night in their own beds. I smiled, remembering all the fun I had when I was a kid. My grandparents were strict, but never raised a hand to me, not even when I needed a good walloping. I didn't like school. Many a time Grandpa had to stand over me to make sure I finished my homework. He even helped with algebra. I had no idea he knew what all those symbols meant. It was Greek to me. I skimmed by with a D. He said he was proud that I hadn't failed. I think the only reason I didn't was because our teacher felt sorry for me.

Russell snored and turned on his side. Even when we camped at Monocle Lake he'd be out like a light while the rest of us were still sitting around the campfire. I thought about what was in store for us. Maybe we'd get lucky and be sent to Germany like Fenders. When he enlisted, the Korean War was over and Viet Nam wasn't like it is today. Fenders was safe in Germany. Then he re-uped and was sent to Fort Carson in Colorado Springs. Maybe we'll stay stateside, too. They don't send every GI to Nam, but we know our chances aren't good. That's why we're expecting the worst. From Detroit we'll fly to Fort Knox for Basic Training. We've never been on a plane, but Flint said there ain't nothing to it. He said just close our eyes and pretend we're sailing on a Great Lakes freighter. He said the clouds will look like fluffy marshmallows. Flint's never been on a plane so he don't know any more about flying than we do, but he tells a good story. Our recruiter said we'd be flying at night so I don't know how many marshmallow clouds we're likely to see.

Time's ticking by. I gotta get some shuteye. The electric clock on my nightstand says it's one-thirty. It was a Christmas gift from Daisy the year we were in tenth grade and started going steady. She'd been my gal for years, but I made it official when we turned sixteen. I didn't have a ring to give her so I bought an ID bracelet with her name and our initials on it. Those bracelets were all the rage. She still wears it as well as my class ring. Behind my closed eyes, I see her as she was when I picked her up for our prom. She was beautiful. Her short brown hair was always a rich color, but I'd never noticed it until she walked into her kitchen. Then I saw how nice it was. She must have done something to her eyelashes, too, because I'd never seen them so curly. She wore a pearl necklace and earrings. Her gown was yellow. She was a vision. When she smiled, I couldn't believe she really loved me, but I knew she did, just like I had loved her from the start.

We lived near each other and one summer afternoon I caught her picking strawberries in the field next to my house. I couldn't have been more than four. Grandpa had given me orders to keep an eye out and not let anyone pick in our field. I grabbed an empty coffee can, crawled underneath the barbed wire fence, and marched up to her. I demanded to know what business she had stealing the berries I was about to pick. Her back was to me. I scared her. When she jumped up, she dropped her glass. Berries rolled everywhere. She started crying and limped away. That's when I saw she had a crooked foot. I told her to stop bawling and asked how come she walked on her ankle. She mumbled something about a cow stepping on her foot when she was a baby and that was why she couldn't walk like other kids. I felt sorry for her and helped her pick up the berries. I told her she could pick all the strawberries she wanted and all the blueberries when they were ripe. From then on, we were best friends. I believed her story about the cow stepping on her ankle. Whenever I went to the barn, I was careful to steer clear of the cows. It was a long time before she told me the truth—that she was born with a club foot.

Prom night we danced to every song. She'd had operations to fix her foot. It was stiff and she couldn't wear high heels like the other girls, but she didn't care. She wore flats that matched her dress. We're about the same height so it was easy for her to rest her head on my shoulder. I never wanted that night to end. Instead of going home when the prom was over, I drove to our special place on Lakeshore Drive. We walked along the beach by Point Iroquois. Waves lapped the shore. When Daisy shivered, I wrapped my jacket around her shoulders. We didn't talk. We knew there was nothing to say that hadn't already been said a million times. Right after graduation I'd be working for Sam's dad. I'd save my wages as a nest egg for a down payment on a house for us. When I had to leave for the Army, I promised to save whatever the government paid me. We'd get wed when the military let me go. Daisy'd be waiting, untouched and pure. She'd have a right to wear a white dress.

A funny thought came to me and I chuckled. We must have been seven or eight when we heard about quicksand. From then on we were convinced there must be some on our land where the soil was boggy. When I told Flint and Johnny what Daisy had read about quicksand, we spent one summer searching for it. Blew and Squeaky joined us. Whenever we came to a damp spot, we got a stick and broke it into pieces. Whoever drew the short piece had to walk into what we thought might be quicksand. After a rain, the mossy ground was soft. When I drew the short piece, I knew for sure I'd be sucked under. The boys promised to go for help, but I knew I'd be dead before they got back. I asked God to forgive me for telling so many lies and promised I'd never lie again. Imagine my surprise when I stepped onto the soft moss and remained standing. The boys laughed until they cried. It was a good joke on me. I went a whole week without telling a lie, but the temptation was too great for me to overcome. I told God I was sorry, but I couldn't keep my promise. He must have understood because I'm still alive. I sure hope I am this time two years from now when I'll get my discharge papers.

I chucked again remembering the time our teacher told us about the great San Francisco earthquake. It destroyed the city and killed thousands of people. We were stupid country hicks. Katie had convinced us an earthquake might strike Chippewa County anytime, and we needed to be prepared. We made plans to save ourselves. We made a pact that as soon as we felt the earth begin to tremble, we'd meet in the middle of Grandpa Marvin's field where there were no trees. We figured we'd be safe because nothing would fall on us. We forgot that the earth opens during a quake and could easily have swallowed us. For weeks afterwards, whenever we heard anything that sounded like a rumbling noise or we thought we felt a slight tremor, we ran towards the field. One evening Mam asked what was going on when I left the supper table and made a dash for the field. She caught me by my belt and demanded an explanation. She didn't laugh when I told her, but she did walk with me to the field where Katie and Johnny were waiting. Then she explained if an earthquake did come our way, it was best to stay home where adults would keep us safe. I've got a lot of good memories and the best grandparents and pals a guy could ever hope for.

Yesterday everyone got together and gave us a royal sendoff. All the gang was there. Danny piled a bunch of our friends into his Chevy, and we had a campfire down by the riverside. It was like old times. Daisy, Elizabeth, Candy, Shirley, and Katie brought the fixings like they used to. Squeaky brought hot dogs, and Rachel baked a chocolate cake. I played my uke, Flint strummed his guitar, and Russell played a harmonica that had belonged to Johnny. His pa gave it to him. He wanted Russell to have it as a reminder of happier days when Johnny was with us. As if we'd ever forget him. Sam and Jill joined us. We laughed when their little tyke, Jimmy, threatened to jump in the river if Sam wouldn't take him fishing the next day. Sam settled down with Jill instead of Jazz. She ran off with a flyboy from the airbase in Kinross. He's stationed somewhere down south. Jill's gonna have another baby. We're betting it's gonna be twins. I think Sam would like that, especially if they're girls. He always was a sucker for a pretty gal. Daughters would have him wrapped around their little fingers.

Eventually I fell asleep. It was six o'clock when Mam knocked on my door. "Time to get up, boys," she said. "Breakfast is ready." It was a strange feeling to be rolling out of bed and getting ready to travel instead of going to the chicken coop and letting out the hens. I shook Russell's shoulder. It took him a minute to realize he wasn't in his own room. We dressed quickly and went downstairs. The table was set with Mam's good china and her best tablecloth, the one she was always going to use at Thanksgiving or Christmas but never did because she was afraid we might spill gravy on it and the stain wouldn't come out. She had lit a fire in the small wood-burning stove in the kitchen. Even in summertime, the mornings were cold enough to keep the fire going for a couple hours. Grandpa Marvin filled our cups with hot coffee while Mam fussed with our plates. She loaded them with all my favorites. Bacon, sausage links, fried onions and potatoes, sunny-side up eggs, three pancakes the size of silver dollars, and plenty of toast. Then she pulled a batch of cinnamon rolls out of the oven. Russell whistled and said he'd never eaten so good, but just like last night, we ate our feast in silence.

When we finished, I walked to the barn with Grandpa. Russell helped Mam with the dishes. When we opened the barn door, we sat on bales of hay opposite each other. As soon as Perkins heard us, she came down from the mow. Old Tom the Third followed her. He was named after a cat that belonged to our neighbor, Mr. Sims. Fenders accidentally shot Old Tom the First during deer season years ago. We promised Sims we'd always name one male cat "Old Tom" in memory of his pet. We kept our word and now every sideroad kid has an Old Tom. Some are known as junior, but mostly we stick to calling them the second, the third, and so on. It's a tradition Daisy said we'll continue when we have kids. I haven't told her I never want them. They ask too many questions, and parents tell too many lies.

The barn was quiet except for the lapping of the cats. Grandpa had brought some milk from the kitchen and poured it into their saucer. We watched them lap every drop then lick their paws as they washed themselves. They jumped in the manger where the sunlight was shining through the window. That's where they'll spend the rest of the day sleeping. The only time they'll stir is if they smell a mouse. That'll be their lunch. We left the barn, but not the memories. I knew I'd take them with me. Everyone was vivid, from the smell of manure to the lowing of the cows to the pitchforks leaning against the wheelbarrow. Although the cows were gone because Grandpa had sold them when the government said all milk had to go directly from the source to a stainless steel holding tank, the milk cans were still there. Hay was in the mangers. The chop boxes that once held sweet feed were empty except for a few oats that would be eaten by mice before the mice were eaten by Perkins or Old Tom the Third.

Russell had put our suitcases in the trunk of Grandpa's car. Mam was dressed in her best gray suit and the hat she wore to church every Sunday. Her black gloves matched her purse and shoes. I'd never noticed how pretty she was. She wasn't old like other grandmothers. Her hair wasn't gray. It was dark brown and wavy. Her face looked young. She had roughed her cheeks and put on lipstick. She was younger than Grandpa Marvin. When she smiled, she was beautiful. "Are you sure you packed everything you'll need?" she asked. I said yes. We didn't need much. The recruiter told us to bring a few things we considered necessary, but not much clothing. Uncle Sam would provide that. I took one last look at the home I might never see again. Mam snapped a picture of me standing by the front steps. Then she snapped one of Russell and me. Then Russell snapped one of Mam and me. Then he snapped one of Mam, Grandpa, and me. Grandpa got behind the driver's seat and honked the horn. It was time to go, but I couldn't leave until I hugged Utah one last time. I heard the camera click as Mam caught Utah licking my face.

The ride to the Soo was awful. I could feel the heaviness in the car. We tried to make conversation, but we all knew the future might be dangerous, if not fatal, for Russell and me. Mam held back her tears as she looked at the mist rising from the river. She said she always loved walking down the road in the early morning hours when the temperature was just right and the mist was coming off the water and rising higher and higher until it disappeared among the treetops.

Grandpa Marvin was more interested in the fields on Six Mile that belonged to his friend, Mansfield Cloves, and were filled with rows of round hay bales waiting to be turned so they could dry underneath before being loaded on the wagons and stacked in Mansfield's mow. He and Grandpa had been friends since their school days. They always helped each other during haying season. The whole Cloves' clan showed up at our house every Christmas. It was the only time Grandpa drank something stronger than water. His limit was one jigger of Peppermint Schnapps. Mam's limit went beyond that. By her third shot, she'd giggle like a schoolgirl. That's when Grandpa would tell her she'd had enough and pour her a cup of coffee. I'd play with the kids. The girls were older, but the two boys were about my age. Now they're at Fort Meade in Maryland.

As we passed underneath the trestle, the Soo Line train was rumbling above us. When I was little, I used to wonder if the rails would collapse and crush us. They never did, of course, but I'm still surprised that old trestle can carry the weight of dozens of box cars. Sometimes Grandpa would pull over to the side of the road and we'd count the number of cars and guess what each one held. When the caboose finally went by, we'd stick our arms out the windows and wave.

Once past the trestle, it wasn't long before we went by Pine Grove Cemetery before turning left on US-2. Whenever I drove my friends to the Soo, Danny would ask me to stop so he could look at the gravestones. They fascinated him and he'd beckon the rest of us guys to walk among them. Some were so old they had sunk in the ground or tipped to one side. Most were tall and it was easy to read the names of the dead. It gave me a strange feeling to know all the people buried underneath the ground had once walked as we had. I didn't like the feelings that stirred in me, especially when a tombstone read the deceased had been killed in a war. Then I'd see a monument that said "infant" and realize that not all who had died had reached adulthood.

"It's a nice morning," Mam said. "No rain predicted for today. I'll wash all the bedding and hang it on the line. When you boys come home on leave, everything will be fresh and clean. Russell, I'm glad you called your parents. How's your father doing?" Mam was in the front seat. She turned to look at Russell who was sitting behind Grandpa.

"About the same. Ma said he had a peaceful night."

"That's good," Mam said. "Blew, did you remember to pack your rosary?"

"Sure did. It's right here in my pocket," I lied. I did pack it, but it was in the bottom of my suitcase.

"Good. Make sure you say it every night."

"I will." That was another lie. I knew Mam would worry so I wanted to ease her mind. As we passed Bell's farm, I saw their Clydesdales in the field, and the cabins in front of the trees north of their house. The cabins were rented to tourists. In the fall, the maples were ablaze with color. It was a beautiful sight, something city people had probably never seen.

The closer we got to the bus station, the quieter we became. Mam stopped talking about who lived where and what groceries she was going to buy when they dropped us off. She also wanted to go to Cowan's Department Store and purchase a gift for Mrs. Cloves' daughter who was getting married in November. The wedding was months away, but Mam was eager to see what new items Cowan's had added to their kitchen department.

We passed the stone mason business, Dorothy's Hamburger joint, and the Emma Nason home for orphans. Then we crossed the Ashumn Street bridge. When Grandpa pulled into the bus station, I was relieved. He opened the trunk and handed Russell his suitcase. I grabbed mine. Mam got out of the car and walked with us to the bus. The driver put our suitcases in the luggage compartment. I turned to my grandparents. "Time to go," I said. "No point hangin' around." We were the last ones to board. The driver had started the bus. Mam hugged me like there was no tomorrow. Grandpa Marvin did the same. Then he shook my hand and slipped a ten spot in it. They both shook hands with Russell. Mam gave him a hug. The driver yelled, "All aboard that's going aboard." We waved goodbye and that was that.

As we drove across the Mackinac Bridge I remembered the first time I crossed the straits in a bus instead of a car driven onto a ferry. It was when the fan bus from Brimley was heading for Lansing and the semi-final basketball games. Our varsity was the best bunch of players in a decade. Everyone was in a great mood on the way home because our team had made it to the finals scheduled for the following Saturday. I was good at football, but rotten when it came to making hoops. I was too short and squat, but Johnny, Danny, Flint, and Squeaky were top players. Flint never missed a free throw. Squeaky never missed a lay-up although he was the shortest player on the team.

Anyway, by the time the game was over, it was dark. After we sang our school song and rehashed the game, the bus got quiet as kids fell asleep. Daisy rested her head on my shoulder. It was about a four-hour drive back home and my shoulder went numb, but I didn't want to shift myself and take a chance of waking her. I imagined how our life together would be. In my mind, I saw us married and doing all the things couples do when they're in love. I even saw us going to the Soo on Friday nights and shopping for groceries at Callaghan's Market on Ashmun. Sounds stupid, I know, but it made me feel good to know I didn't have to wonder what my future looked like. I had no doubt it would be filled with laughter. I thought I might even change my mind about not having kids. It might be fun to have a miniature Daisy running around chasing a miniature Blew, but I wouldn't want more than two kids unless we didn't get a girl on both tries. If we were going to have children, I would demand a daughter no matter how many tries it took. I laughed out loud at the memory and awakened Russell.

"What's so funny?" he asked. "Where are we?" He rubbed his eyes and looked around.

"I was thinkin' about the past," I said. "I don't know where we are. The last sign I saw said we were forty-nine miles from Detroit. Go back to sleep. I'll poke you awake when we get there." The drive was a long one because we stopped at every little burg from Sault Ste. Marie to Detroit. Seemed like we just pulled out of one small town and a minute later we were pulling into a Greyhound station in another. When we arrived in Detroit, I nudged Russell.

"Are we here?" he asked.

"Yeah, we're here alright," I said. People were gathering things from their seats and beginning to leave the bus. Some women didn't have much except big purses and paper bags. A few old Black men didn't carry anything. On our last stops we had picked up folks who must have been visiting their kin judging by the light way they traveled. A feller about my height stopped at our seat and motioned us to go ahead. His face was peppered with freckles almost as red as his hair. The guy behind him was his duplicate.

"You boys goin' our way?" I asked.

"If you're going to war, I guess we are," he said. "Next stop Viet Nam if we're lucky." He laughed.

"Lucky," I said as we walked down the steps. The noise of the city blasted in my ears. "What'd you mean by that?"

"It's this way. If me or my brother gets killed, Ma gets a check for $10,000. That's what the Army values a man's life at. Ten thousand bucks. Ain't much, but it'd keep Ma going for the rest of her life." He shook my hand, grabbed a knapsack, and went across the station to catch another bus. I didn't get his name, but it didn't matter. Like the rest of us, from now on he'd just be a nameless number. Our recruiter met us and put us on a bus heading for the airport. We were beginning a journey that would take us only God knew where, but we were ready. By the time we reached the airport, it was almost dusk. We boarded the TWA. When the steps were pulled up and the plane took off, it wasn't Russell who fell asleep. It was me. I missed seeing those marshmallow clouds Flint was so sure were there. Maybe I'll get a chance on the homebound flight. I hope so.

Daisy

I kept every letter Blew wrote. They're a precious gift I'll always treasure. As I read each one, I feel close to him. Shirley, I'm going to share some with you. Not the ones that are personal and meant only for my eyes. I'll never share those with anyone. The letters here will give you an idea of what it was like for him. He told me he rarely wrote to any of the sideroad kids so perhaps he never wrote to you. You never mentioned getting any from him. These aren't very interesting, but I'm sure they're typical of what most soldiers wrote home so as not to scare their loved ones. I hope I'm doing the right thing. Give me a call when you have time, and if you're in Brimley when I'm here, let's get together for coffee and a long chat.

* * *

Dear Daisy,

15 Aug 68: I'm doing fine. About eight other fellows flew from Detroit to Fort Knox. We were at the reception station for three weeks. We haven't seen anyone we know, but some of the guys from Brimley might show up when we start Basic Training. I tried to call you last night, but nobody answered. I sure hope you weren't running around with one of the flyboys. Just kidding. I know you were probably at a bingo game. We haven't gotten our uniforms yet. When we get our pictures taken, I'll send you one. You'll see how handsome I am in my dress greens.

There ain't much to do while we wait for Basic to begin. We pick up whatever's on the ground and do other make work chores. One day we paint something green, and the next day we paint it red just to pass the time while waiting for our battalion to get full. I don't know what that means, but I do know once Basic starts we'll have to take classes and learn about military stuff. I'll miss your help when I don't remember what I read in the books.

I just bummed a couple envelopes from the guy who has the bunk under mine. We laughed. We've written more letters to the folks back home than we've written in the past fifteen years. Tonight I go on what's called "fire watch." It's only for an hour from eleven o'clock to midnight then one of the guys will relieve me. We have to watch for fire in the barracks and for people stealing stuff. Glad I didn't bring anything worth money or it might be gone the minute I turned my back. I'm gonna hit the hay. Will write again soon.

18 Sept 68: They let us sleep in today. We got up at 7 and ate breakfast. It was pretty good. There's guys here from all over the states. Some speak with such a heavy drawl, I can't understand them. The colored guys speak a language all their own. I usually have no idea what they're saying, but so far nobody's been in a fight. Our barracks have almost as many white guys as colored ones. Tomorrow we'll get up at 5. We have to make our beds and they have to be just so or the Drill Sergeant will make us give him 25 push-ups.

I learned today they'll train me in operating heavy equipment. It's what I wanted and was promised, but you never know with the Army. They put you where they want you. I also got all my uniforms so I'll be sending my civilian clothes home. We're not allowed to wear them during Basic. I also got my hair cut. I lost all my long, thick hair and now I look bald just like all the other guys. This will be a quick note until later.

21 Sept 68: They moved us out of the reception station's old barracks and into new ones three stories high. Ours was only half-full until a couple days ago when about 50 more guys got here. Russell's on the second story. I'm on the third. I don't see him as often as I thought I would cause we're in different squads in our platoon. We have to keep our areas neat. Even the dust has a certain place to settle. Haha. I saw four guys from home. They were coming in just as we were leaving the reception station. These barracks are nice. We have wall lockers and foot lockers. My address is Pvt. Bernard Sullivan, Co. B, 15th Bn, 4th Tng Bde, VSATC, Armor, Fort Knox, KY 40121. It's a long address. I won't bother telling you what it stands for. At the bottom of the envelope write 4th Platoon and underline it. That way I'll be sure to get your letters. I'll be here for about a month, so write as often as you can. We're in formation for mail call. The guys will be envious if I get letters every day. Well, gotta go. It's nine o'clock and lights out time. I can just hear Grandpa Marvin yelling, douse the lights. Only difference is he wouldn't make me give him push-ups if I was slow in turning them off.

24 Sept 68: Today we had a few classes on different Army regulations and stuff like that. We also did some marching and drilling. We didn't actually drill for anything like oil. Army drills mean learning how to get into formation which means standing in lines. It's too hard to explain all of it. I'll tell you what clothes Uncle Sam issued me. 1 OD (olive drab) duffel bag, 2 cotton trouser webbing belts, 1 pair black leather combat boots, 1 black web belt buckle, 1 AG-344 wool garrison cap, 2 OG-106 utility polyester caps, 5 pairs OG cotton drawers, 5 OG handkerchiefs, 1 insignia branch of service, 2 insignia U.S., 2 cotton khaki short sleeve shirts, 1 OG-107 utility fatigue, 1 pair black leather dress oxford, 3 pairs cotton black socks, 5 pairs cushion sole socks, 3 OG bath towels, 1 pair OG-107 utility fatigue trousers, 2 pairs cotton khaki trousers, 5 OG cotton ¼ length sleeve undershirt, 1 cotton and nylon OG-107 field jacket coat, and 1 AG-274 taupe raincoat. Did you ever think I'd be able to list all the clothes I owned? Haha. Not that I had that many when I was home, but ain't this a hoot? I thought you'd like to know how generous Uncle Sam is. Imagine. Five pairs of drawers (underwear!) and five undershirts. Looks like I'll be doing a wash once a week. Love, *Blew*

30 Sept 68: There's over 300 guys from Michigan here at the Fort. There's quite a few in our company and seven or eight in our platoon. They're mostly from Detroit, Bay City, and other towns bigger than Brimley. This evening I go on detail with about nine other guys. We have to clean up some rooms. Nothing but sweep, sweep, sweep. We're gonna have a big inspection. We've been here long enough so they're giving us Post privileges which means this weekend we can go anywhere we want to on Post. We'll wear our dress greens and get free time from Saturday noon until Sat. evening then from Sunday morning to Sun. night.

There ain't much new to report, Daisy. We went to the rifle range today. I shot about 48 rounds at pop-up targets. It was raining and I didn't do as good as I could have. For supper we had steaks and French fries. Pretty good, but most anything would taste good after being out all day and eating chop suey for lunch in the rain. We have KP every 4th day. I've had it twice. I've been lucky. The new guys get it as soon as they get here. Guess what? I finally got my first paycheck—$46.00! As Fenders would say, don't spend it all in one place! Nighty night. Love, *Blew*

10 Oct 68: Today I got three letters from you, one from Mam, two from Elizabeth, and one from Flint's Aunt Ida. What a haul! I didn't have time to read any of them until after we had record fire. That means instead of practicing our rifles we were actually supposed to hit the targets. I got marksmen which is the lowest you can make and pass. I'll get a ribbon pinned on my dress green jacket. I'm happy just to get enough to earn a ribbon. If I was a better shot, they might change their minds and send me to the infantry. I just finished reading your letter. I'm glad you're enjoying your college classes. I knew you would. You're a smart gal. I sure am glad you're mine.

1 Nov 68: Sorry I haven't written in a few weeks. It's been awful busy here. I finished Basic. We marched miles and miles. I sure am glad I'm in the 1st squad. That means all the guys behind us get to eat our dust, and believe me, there's plenty of dust to eat! We did day and night maneuvers which means we pretended to find and track the enemy. The Drill shot blanks and we dropped where we were. Sometimes that meant in a ditch, but they gotta train us to face anything. I didn't mind bivouac. Fenders probably had the same thing. We camped in the woods for a week, ate C-rations, washed our face and hands in our helmets, slept in tents, and ran an obstacle course. I almost didn't make it over the 6-foot fence. We had to run through the course, crawl underneath barbed wire, and scale the wooden fence. Took me a couple tries. One of the guys ran around it. You should have heard the Drill. He screamed bloody murder. When they herded us into a cabin and let loose the gas, my mask had a hole in it. I flailed my arms and motioned to my mask. It was only when I fell the Drill dragged me out. I laid on the ground until I could breathe again. He didn't send me back in like he did some of the other guys.

Every day when we shoot, we have to break down our rifles and clean them. We're up at 4:15, dress fast, make our beds, and stand in formation by 5. They check our uniforms for strings and dirt and hair and anything else they can find. They call them IOs. If we're not shaved and dressed to perfection, the Drill makes us do push-ups. If he finds something two days in a row, we do them with one hand. Luckily, I inspect myself before formation.

Did I tell you I've gained five pounds? Nobody ever heard of anybody gaining weight in Basic, not with all the marching we do, but the chow is so darn (oops) good, Daisy, I eat twice what I normally would. They won't give me another set of fatigues so I'm glad I can still squeeze into mine, but I'm gonna have to stop eating dessert and you know how much I love dessert! They always have pies and cakes and we can take as much as we want. Breakfast is bacon, eggs, sausage, pancakes, fried potatoes, and buckets of coffee. We had ribs last night for supper. Russell sat next to me. You should have seen him eating them. The sauce was running down his arms and as fast as he cleaned one rib, he reached for another. They were good, but the best part was watching him eat. We're in different platoons so we don't get together much. For my AIT, they're sending me to Fort Leonard Wood in Missouri for more training. That's where the Army's engineering school is. I'll learn to clear bush military style to make roads, something I'll be doing if they send me to Nam. Russell's going to Fort Benning in Georgia.

* * *

I hadn't heard from Blew in two months and was beyond myself with worry. He was good to write often. I couldn't imagine what had happened. Two days before Christmas Mom said someone was at the door to see me. I thought it was Katie home for the holidays. I nearly fainted when it was Blew who was standing before me. He was on leave before being sent to Viet Nam. I couldn't believe my eyes. Standing before me was the handsomest guy I'd ever seen. My Blew had grown into a man. He looked like a million dollars. When he held out his arms, I collapsed against him. I'd never known such happiness.

We talked for hours. He told me everything that had happened in the months he'd been gone and answered all my questions. He explained he didn't have time to define every term I asked about and apologized for not doing so. I told him it didn't matter. That I had asked Dad and he explained as much as he remembered from his time in the Army. I told Blew I didn't care about anything except that he was home and we'd spend every hour together or at least as many as my parents would allow.

That Christmas was the most wonderful of my life. On Christmas Eve we went to midnight mass with all our friends, Catholic or otherwise. We wanted to be together. The church was beautifully decorated. Two large spruce trees sparkled with at least one-hundred lights. Afterwards everyone gathered at our house. Mom had prepared a meal. We ate and talked until four in the morning. Nobody wanted to go home. Blew told us not to worry about him. That he would be okay during the year he'd spend in Nam. I was so proud of him. When my parents went to bed and our friends went home, Blew added more wood to the fire. We sat on the davenport and watched the flames as they reached higher and higher. Blew adjusted the damper and they settled down.

We were tired. Blew put his arm around me, and I rested my head against his shoulder. The only light in the living room came from the fireplace and our tree. Everything looked magical. The drapes were open and the outside light was on. Suddenly the moon appeared from behind the clouds. We looked out the window and watched snowflakes drifting down. It was like a scene from a Christmas card. The radio was on and WSOO was playing Christmas carols. I didn't want the dawn to break. I wanted everything to stay as it was. I didn't want to think about a faraway country where soldiers were fighting a war they hadn't started and didn't want to be in. I buried my face in Blew's shoulder.

After Christmas, the days melted into each other as silently as snowflakes covered the ground. Each day, each hour was more precious than the last. It meant one minute closer to the time when Blew would have to leave. We held ourselves together as best we could. We arranged snowmobile rides, outdoor campfires on the riverbank, going to the movies at the Soo Theatre, and talking until dawn. Sometimes the adults joined us and the men told stories of great heroism they had seen during their time in war. The women cooked delicious meals and made dozens of desserts. Everyone showered Blew with love.

Russell was also on leave and one day he came from Eckerman and visited us. Squeaky gave Rachel an engagement ring, and we threw an impromptu party for them. Elizabeth showed off her latest boyfriend, a flyboy from the airbase in Kinross. Katie was home from Michigan State and Danny from Michigan Tech. They were with us almost every day. Shirley joined us as often as she could. She was taking care of her dad and grandmother while her mother was hospitalized. Larry was the only one of our group who was missing. He had enlisted in the Marines right after graduation and was killed five days after stepping off the plane in Nam.

The morning arrived when it was time for Blew to leave. Everyone wanted to drive to the airport and see him off, but he said no. He didn't want his last memory of home to be one of a bunch of crybabies. He said if we promised to laugh and cheer and raise a glass to victory and his safe return, we could drive behind his Pontiac, but only I would ride with him. Everyone agreed. Eight cars followed us as we drove down the sideroad, crossed the bridge, and turned right on Six Mile. Blew laughed and said it was the first time he'd ever led a parade, and he liked it. The nearer we got to the airport, the more we laughed and joked and remembered silly things we'd done as children. When we turned in the parking lot, all the cars lined up next to us. Blew grabbed his duffel bag, gave his grandparents one last hug, kissed me and wiped away my tears. He yelled a goodbye to his friends who were hooting and hollering well wishes, and then he turned and entered the small terminal. Within minutes we watched as he walked to the prop plane that would take him to Detroit where he'd board a jet heading for California. Another change of planes and he'd be in Hawaii to refuel. His final stop would be an airbase in Viet Nam. My heart broke as I waved until the plane disappeared into the clouds.

* * *

7 Jan 69: I arrived at the reception station in Oakland about 11:30 p.m. today. Believe me, I was beat. I found my duffle bag right off the bat at the San Francisco airport. It was in the lost and found department. I had no trouble getting it from them. Then I caught a bus right to the front door of the reception station. We were issued our jungle fatigues and had a lot of paperwork to fill out. It was after 1:30 a.m. before I got to bed. It's now 6:45 a.m. I think we have an hour or two then we're off to a part of the world I could do without seeing. Haha. Just a couple more hours and I'll be on a jet to Hawaii. From there we go to Guam and then on to Nam. They say it takes about 22 hours to get there. We'll be in Hawaii for about 90 minutes and the same in Guam. I doubt if we'll be able to look around, but I'll try to take a few pictures and get some postcards.

I don't know exactly where I'm going. Wherever my unit is sent. Somebody said we'll be in the Northern part. I haven't seen anybody from my class at Leonard Wood, but I have seen a few guys from other companies in dozer operations. From what they say, I'll have it pretty good over there. I'm getting a little drowsy so will try and get some sleep. We're in something like barracks with lots of bunks and guys. Bye for now. P.S. Don't worry, okay? Love you.

12 Jan 69: Well, we landed at Bien Hao Air Base. I finally made it to my unit after a long wait and a lot of plane rides. I'm somewhere south of Saigon. Dong Tam is the name. I don't think I spelled it right, but it doesn't matter. The guy from my old class is in the next company—D—but I don't know how far away that is. I have a pretty good deal. I'm with the construction engineers. I'll be operating a tractor. It's pretty hot here, not like home where you're wearing a winter coat and watching snow fall! They say it will get much hotter as time passes. I'll go to chow in a few minutes, but first there's mail call in my room. At least we call it a room, but it's not much. No door, four or five guys, and the hallway goes right through 2 bunks on each side of the wall. That does it for now, Daisy. I'll write again soon. Don't worry. Everything's fine. Love you.

16 Jan 69: Today I operated a No. 2 shovel all day, but tomorrow I'll be on a tractor. We work about 12 hours a day for 6½-7 days a week. Dong Tam is my base camp. It's a nice place—no trouble with the Viet Cong—only saw a couple in the PW camp on base and that was all. We might go a few miles away in a month or two to work on an airstrip. Some guys say it's even better there than here. It's by the Cambodia border. I'm in the Mekong Delta area which is good so don't worry. The news on TV doesn't mean much so don't put too much faith in it. Take my word for it. Everything is just fine. My outfit, the 93rd Engineers, says they haven't lost a man to the enemy in two years so that sounds good. Write as often as you can and tell me all the news. Love you.

24 Jan 69: You'd laugh if you could see me. My chest and shoulders are starting to peel and I'm getting almost as dark as the locals. It's raining now. I have some time off today so will get caught up on writing letters. Yesterday I was barracks orderly. All I had to do was sweep the floor and make sure nobody came in and stole anything. It took about an hour to get things in shape. There's a guy in the barracks from Grand Rapids. He gets the paper. There was a write-up about the Soo Locks in it. It sure seemed strange to be reading about home as I sat on my bunk in Nam. Send me some clippings of what's happening. Stuff like who's getting married, who died, stuff like that. Sure would make me feel close to you. Love you.

12 Feb 69: Nothing new to report, Daisy. I know you like to hear from me so you know I'm still alive. I promise I'm fine. The food is pretty good. Only bad thing is the flies! They're on everything. Mam would have a fit if she could see them. Today I had KP. I started at 6 a.m. and quit two hours later when the Vietnamese people came in to do the work. Then I was back on KP at 4:30 until about 7:30 p.m. It's a good system. This will make you laugh. Mrs. Odell sent me some packets of iced tea. I hate the stuff! In the mess hall we have different kinds of Kool-Aid and lots of iced tea. I never touch it! Here's some good news. I got my license to drive a 5-ton truck. The land is swampy and there's a river by the airfield, but I haven't seen much land other than around the camp. It's mostly just swamp. Mosquitoes and flies by the hundreds. Gotta go now. Love you.

27 Feb 69: For the last couple days I've been working in the motor pool on a 5-ton water truck. It's going to be scrapped for junk and we'll get a new one. I got two letters from you. Thanks for the pictures. You look great. I've got to buy an album because it's so hot and humid here the pics stick together. Did I tell you I bought a new radio for $25? It's a big one that uses batteries. If you feel like it, I sure would like a box of your famous peanut butter cookies and maybe some date ones. Don't send banana bread or anything like that. It will rot before it gets here. Mam sent some envelopes, but I couldn't open them because the glue had stuck them closed. I wrote and told her to send the kind that has the strip to pull off. I threw the other ones away. It takes about a week to get your letters. Love you.

17 Mar 69: Today I was moved to a place called Tan An about 20 miles north of Dong Tam. It's not as neat, and there's a lot more mud. I've seen lots of rice patties and people along the way, but no sign of the VC. I was sent here to operate a "bob-tail" which is a tractor without a scraper on the back. I'll be spending my time rolling and packing the dirt and pulling machines out of the mud when they get stuck. My address will still be the same, but it'll take longer for my letters to reach you. Mail here is moved by convoy to and from Dong Tam. Happy St. Patrick's Day! I almost forgot about that because one day is the same as the next over here. Love you.

8 Apr 69: I met a guy from Detroit and he reminded me of Mr. Quails. He's about the same size. I laughed when he talked about crossing the Mac Bridge for the first time. Said he was white-knuckled until he reached St. Ignace. It was funny because he's as black as coal. There's three different projects going on here so they're bringing in more men. They're building a barracks and rolling dirt that's hauled away by truck. Forms being made, concrete being poured and lots of other stuff just like a regular construction site except for the helicopters. They're everywhere. That's one reason why the VC never come close. There's no cover for them just rice patties. So far I haven't heard any rifle fire so don't worry. There's a small chapel at another part of our camp which consists of different sections including Seabees (soldiers with construction skills and medical aid), Infantry, and Engineers. Love you.

* * *

That was the last letter I shared with Shirley. From early April onward, Blew's letters all read the same. He never wrote anything about the war. It was as if he was shielding it from us. Everybody worried about him. His letters told us he had it made and the food was good. I didn't know what to believe. Every night on the news we saw nothing but death and destruction, yet Blew always said everything was fine. Sometimes I wouldn't hear from him for a month. That's when I'd panic, but then one day I'd get a batch of letters. He explained there had been some trouble with mail pick-up, but he didn't say what kind of trouble. The last few letters I received were written in June, July, and August during the rainy season when he said the engineers weren't as busy building roads as they were getting stuck in the mud.

He asked me to send him rolls of color film but no more than twelve exposures and to write DO NOT X-RAY—FILM on the outside of the package. He said to make it a small package because if it was a large one, they would x-ray it for sure. I didn't know what that meant, but I supposed x-raying would ruin the film. In one letter he said he might be put on a water pump to drain a rice patty to construct more buildings. He wrote they had moved him to Ben Luc, twenty-six miles south of Saigon and twenty-five miles north of Tan An. He said they took their meals at a Navy camp. He was worried about Russell who was north of his camp where the North Vietnamese Regulars were. He never mentioned anything about the guys from Brimley who were killed. When we saw a notice in the newspaper, one of us would send him the clipping, but I didn't. I thought it would depress him. Some of the guys he knew from Basic Training and engineering school had probably been killed, but either he didn't know or he never told us. It was awful letting him know that one of our classmates, Howard, drowned himself when he got orders to report for duty. Although they weren't best friends, the sideroad kids had known Howard since kindergarten. We think what happened was he didn't want to disappoint his father who worked at the Pentagon or his grandfather who was a retired Army general.

By September, Blew had been in Viet Nam nine months. His letters were fewer and fewer. In every one he mentioned the number of days he had left in Southeast Asia. He couldn't leave Nam until January unless the Army decided to send him back to the states before his year over there was up. In October his unit was sent to Camp Viking northwest of Da Nang. Blew said they were to be on permanent guard, and they were miles from a PX. He asked me to send him a birthday card so he could send it to his grandmother. And he said he was going to make Sp/4 which meant more money to save for our wedding.

Over the next months, his letters were identical. He talked about the rain giving way to cooler days and fewer bugs, the work he was doing on clearing the jungle to make roads, the cold beers the guys enjoyed, and the meals. I continued to write every day, telling him about my college classes and what the neighbors were up to. I knew he was counting the days when he'd be stateside again. Although he never said it, I could tell he was homesick. He still had a year left to serve, but it would be in the states. He was being sent to Fort Jackson in South Carolina. He thought it was crazy. He was in the engineers. He didn't know why they were sending him there. He was hoping to get stationed closer to Michigan and continue doing construction work.

The last letter he sent his grandmother was a week before he left Nam. He told her to put a case of beer in the fridge and a carton of ice cream in the freezer. He said they were working twelve-hour days, and he hadn't received any mail in ten days which was unusual. He said he would write one last letter to me. Then he added a P.S. and said he had received seventeen letters in one day. Within two weeks of receiving his last letter, he boarded a TWA jet that brought him home. When he held me, I had no words. My Blew had changed. The little boy I'd fallen in love with all those years ago was gone. The man who replaced him was almost unrecognizable. It was then I realized what his time in Viet Nam had done to him.

While home on leave, he drank all the time. We spent hours together, but we didn't make plans for the future. We were like strangers. He was lost in whatever abyss Viet Nam had placed him in. I was as patient as I could be, but I didn't know what to do or say. He drove too fast, drank too much, and smoked weed. I was concerned he wanted to call off our engagement but was afraid to ask. I didn't want to know the answer. All kinds of thoughts ran through my mind. I convinced myself he had met someone and wanted his freedom but didn't want to hurt me. He knew I would be sad. What he didn't know was that I could accept whatever decision he made. I loved him, of course, but I had moved beyond our small circle of friends. College opened new doors for me. I was active in various clubs and attended social gatherings I never would have thought possible. If Blew no longer wanted to marry me, I would be sad, but it wouldn't be the end of the world that it once would have been. I was even considering applying to Trinity College in Dublin.

The night before he was to leave, he was coming down the hill when he lost control of his car. Either he was too drunk to know what he was doing or he hit an icy patch. Either way, the car left the road and landed in the river. The ice wasn't thick enough to hold its weight. Sam heard a loud noise and ran to see what was happening. He saw the taillights disappear and called the authorities.

Blew's body was still in the car when they pulled it out of the river. When the wake and funeral were over, I took the money from our joint account and gave it to his grandparents. We talked for a long time. They brought out the photo album and showed me pictures of Blew when he was a baby. I told them about our first meeting and how he had yelled at me and told me to stop picking his strawberries. We laughed, we cried, we hugged, and I promised to visit them often. As I was leaving, they handed me the cash, but I said I didn't want it. It was for our future, and since we didn't have one, I wanted them to keep it. After much explaining why they didn't want his savings and that his pay really belonged to me, we decided to put it towards a beautiful granite tombstone.

As I walked home that afternoon, the sun broke through the clouds. Its rays turned the snow-covered field, where Blew and I first met, into a glorious meadow of sparkling diamonds. I knew everything was going to be okay. Blew and all the other boys, who had died in the war zone or as a result of it, were safe now. Their spirits had found the peace that eluded them in battle. I brushed away the tears threatening to freeze on my face. I knew I would never forget the sweet little boy who had chased me from his berry patch and then stole my heart all those years ago.

For a long time afterwards I wondered what thoughts had gone through his mind when he became aware that he couldn't get out of the car and was going to go down with it. I wondered if he thought of me or his grandparents or his best buddies who had died serving their country or if he had thought of anything at all as the car sank. I wondered what it's like to know you're going to die and there's nothing you can do about it. I wondered if he saw Johnny and if he had told him he had changed his mind, but it was too late because he had kicked the milk stool out from underneath his feet and the rope around his neck choked him. I wondered what other spirits he saw and if they had guided him through the gates of heaven. I was sure that the mother and father he had never known on earth were there to welcome him home.

Flint

"I'm telling you, Candy, you'd be sitting on top of the world if you had married me instead of that no-good airman. Didn't I warn you he wasn't worth the dust on your shoes? What were you thinking? But it's not too late. Marry me." I'm sitting in the living room of Uncle Leo's house in Rudyard. Candy's standing before the fireplace. Her back is to me and she's crying like a newborn kitten.

"It won't work, Flint. I'm no good. I'd cheat on you," she said.

"That's crazy talk and you know it."

"I'm just trying to be honest."

I was disgusted. I got up and threw another log on the fire. Uncle Leo and Candy's daughters, Missy and Dotty, walked into the room. The girls were carrying trays filled with an assortment of cookies they had baked and brought over. My uncle was carrying mugs of hot cocoa.

"Have you two decided on a wedding date yet?" he asked. He sat in the orange recliner next to the fireplace and put his feet on the ottoman. He leaned back and looked at me. "Well?" He was anxious for me to marry Candy. He said then he'd have the family he always wanted but fate had stolen from him. I watched Candy as she twisted the ring on her finger. It was an old one Aunt Ida had given me when I was thirteen. I gave it to Candy the night we had our last campfire on the banks of our river. That was years ago. She must care for me. Otherwise, she'd have thrown the ring away.

"We're working on it," I said. The room was flooded with the sound of Christmas music the girls had insisted must be played while they decorated the tree, the mantle, and the baluster. Then Missy lit the pine candles on the mantle. The smell of pine was strong, but not unpleasant. Dotty pushed Uncle Leo's feet aside and sat on the ottoman. She stroked Crank, our hound dog. The scene before my eyes was one of tranquility. It belied the undercurrent of melancholy that seemed to perpetually surround Candy, but she had pulled herself together and was ready to join in the fun. Brenda Lee's famous Christmas song came on the radio. I grabbed her hand, and we started dancing. Missy and Dotty did likewise. Uncle Leo clapped. Crank howled.

When the song ended and we collapsed on the couch, I said our friends would soon be arriving for a hayride. The girls were delighted. Since the first snowfall, they had been asking when I was going to fix Uncle Leo's sleigh and hitch it to the horses. I said never because the sleigh was old and broken and the horses were tired. I didn't tell them the hay wagon was in good shape and the tractor never tired. It was ready to go regardless of the weather. Yesterday I piled bales of hay on the wagon then spread loose hay on the floor and hitched the Case to it. The snow's not deep, so I won't have any trouble driving the tractor around the fields and down the roads. Candy looked my way and smiled. The air around me felt lighter as if it sensed something oppressive had gone.

"Girls," she said. "We better go home. You're going to need warmer clothes. What time do you want us back, Flint?"

"About three." They gathered their coats and hats and kissed Uncle Leo's cheek. The room was awfully quiet when the door closed behind them. Even Crank must have felt a change in the atmosphere. He lowered his head and moved closer to the fire.

"You gonna marry that girl?" Uncle Leo asked. He lit a cigarette and slowly blew smoke rings. They disappeared and he blew more. It's funny how things turn out. As I looked around the room, I remembered how much I had wanted my own home to look like this. Our house was a shack. Always had been and I figured it always would be, but Pops came home when he got word I was in Nam. I guess he thought if I was killed, he'd get a piece of the money the Army would have paid Ma. But I didn't die and Pops got no money, but he got a whole lot more. He got ambition. I don't know whether it was Ma's drinking or my sisters' bellyaching that changed him, but Pops was hired at the Soo Locks and pulled line. He made enough money to fix up the house. Now he and Ma live in comfort and laugh about the old days. She still likes her rhubarb wine, and he still likes to roam, but nowadays he goes no farther than Rudyard and stops by here for his second breakfast.

Uncle Leo and Pops became friends. They rehash the days of their youth. I've heard stories I never would have believed when I was a kid. Stories about how they used to play at dances in the surrounding areas. Pops on guitar and Uncle Leo on the violin. Aunt Ida ran off with her fancy man shortly after I left for the Army. My uncle told Pops I'd inherit this farm and when I came home he wanted me to move in and start running things. I think Pops was glad I wouldn't be underfoot and giving him orders. Things do work out no matter how bleak they seem at the time.

The sun broke through the clouds, filling the room with rays filtering through the lace curtains the way they did in our front room. When I was a kid, I'd watch the patterns they made on the floor and how they'd change when the wind blew the branches on the trees outside the windows. I got the same feeling now that I had in my youth. Something stirred inside me. Something that was good. I looked at my uncle. He had fallen asleep. I took the cigarette from his fingers and ground it out in an ashtray. Crank lifted his head. I put another piece of maple on the fire.

It was still early, just half-past one. I took the photo album from the bookshelf. All the pictures were in black and white and held in place by little black triangles glued to the pages. I didn't know most of the people looking at me. They were Aunt Ida's kinfolk who had stayed in Finland or Norway or some other cold country in Europe. On the last pages were several pictures of Blew and me. I miss him and still feel his presence when I'm working in one of the sheds. Sometimes I hear his voice when I'm asleep. I always thought we'd be business partners with Johnny. I remember the summer of 1958. We called it our summer of discovery. A clerk at Woolworths had once told me I was a planner. At the time, I didn't know what she meant, but during that summer I realized I was a planner and a dang good one.

"Anybody home?" I heard Katie's voice as she opened the kitchen door. "Flint, where are you?"

"In here," I yelled. I closed the album, put it back on the shelf, and walked to the kitchen. Katie was taking off her coat and scarf. Her boots were on the rug. She was shaking snowflakes from her hair.

"What smells so good? The coffee?" she asked. Without waiting for answers, she reached for the pot on the stove and took a cup from the cupboard. "Where's the good stuff?" she asked meaning where's the brandy. She sat at the table and spooned sugar into her cup. I handed her the bottle. She poured some into her coffee. As she raised the cup to her lips, she pushed her long, wavy brown hair from her face. "Are you going to talk?" she asked. Her aqua eyes burrowed into my brown ones. Her beauty was overwhelming. She couldn't see it. She couldn't see anything good about herself. After Johnny died she made friends with the Christian Brothers and all their relatives. How she managed to function when half-drunk was a mystery to me.

"When are you gonna bring your fellow home for us to give him the once over?" I asked. She worked in U.S. Senator Riegle's Detroit office. Every summer she brought someone home and told us this was the guy she was gonna marry, but every Christmas she came home alone. This year was no different. After she graduated from Michigan State University and joined the Peace Corps, we wondered if she'd marry one of the locals from Bolivia, but no, she didn't bring anyone home when she left South America. "Well? Who's the latest guy in your life?" I asked again. She smiled and shook her head.

"No guy this year. I'm tired of the dating game. Maybe I'll come home and marry you." We laughed. "If Candy knew she had competition, she'd get you to the altar tomorrow," she said.

"If only," I said. Katie put her elbows on the table and stared into my eyes. I knew what was coming because she asked the same question every time she came home.

"Why didn't I give Johnny hope? Why was I bullheaded? I feel so guilty." She reached for my hands and squeezed them.

"You were young," I said. "We all feel guilty. He fooled everyone, even his pa, but life goes on, Katie."

"I know. I keep waiting for the pain to go away but when I come home, I feel it stronger than ever. It's around every corner of this road. Every building. It's everywhere. Sometimes I think I'll go crazy if I stay here longer than a few days. Honestly, Flint, I hate coming home."

"Don't say that, Katie. Grief doesn't have an expiration date like a carton of eggs."

"Stupid, isn't it, that stuff now has a pre-determined shelf life? Remember when we were kids? There was no such thing as an expiration date on anything. It's a wonder we survived." She laughed and poured more brandy into her cup.

"I remember everything about our childhood. Sometimes it seems like yesterday. Sometimes an eternity ago." Katie nodded. She reached for the Christmas catalog on the table and thumbed through it. The wind blew hard against the north side of the house. It was much stronger than it had been when I did the morning chores. The sky was clear then. Now snow was beginning to fall. I watched as Squeaky parked his truck alongside Katie's car. He jumped out of the driver's side and ran around to open Rachel's door. She handed him one of the twins. Must be Holly. Squeaky would never allow a pink hat on Henry. "Katie, look who's here." She joined me at the window.

"It's hard to believe," she said. "Squeaky a father. Look how tenderly he holds the baby."

"Maybe it's time you thought about settling down and having one of your own," I said. When she responded, her voice was soft as cotton candy and so low I could barely hear it.

"No, Flint. Marriage and children are not in my future." I didn't say anything. What was there to say? She seemed so frail, so broken. She put on a good show, but I knew her well enough to know she was hurting. Rachel and Squeaky came in. Squeaky held a twin in each arm.

"Let the fun begin," he yelled. "These two rascals are ready for a hayride." He dropped Henry in Katie's lap and handed Holly to me. The kids wiggled free and ran across the floor. Before Rachel had a chance to remove their snowsuits and boots, they were jumping on Crank and having a grand time.

It wasn't long before Elizabeth and Shirley showed up. As usual, Elizabeth was complaining about the cold, and Shirley had brought enough food to feed an army. She preheated the oven and put the turkey in to keep it warm. Soon Danny and Millie arrived. Candy returned with her girls, and I said it was time to go if we wanted to miss the storm that was coming in off Lake Superior. We headed outside. The wind was getting stronger and snow was coming down at a good rate, but nobody wanted to call off the ride. Everyone piled in and bundled up with blankets they had brought. I started the Case and we were off.

I drove through the field then turned on the road leading to Koski's. Shirley insisted we make his house our first stop. She had baked a pumpkin pie for him. He doesn't farm anymore or do much of anything. He's become a hermit and doesn't like being disturbed, but that doesn't stop Shirley from giving him homemade food. She treats old people as kindly as her pets. I drove down his lane and stopped. Shirley jumped out, banged on his front door and yelled "Merry Christmas." When he stuck his head out, she handed him the pie and promised to return with a plate filled with turkey and all the trimmings. Before Koski could argue, she was back on the wagon. Everybody yelled a holiday greeting before he closed the door. I turned the tractor around and headed west on Ploegstra Road. We had a few more stops before I returned to our fields.

By the time we got back, everybody was ready for hot cocoa and the warmth of the fireplace. The gals ran for the house. The fellows stayed behind and unhitched the wagon when I backed it into the pole barn. Then I parked the tractor next to it. Danny took a flask from his pocket and passed it around. The whiskey felt good as it warmed my throat. We don't see much of him since he took a job with Boeing on the west coast, but when he does come home, he always buys the best booze and stops by the farm. Other than being richer than the rest of us, he hasn't changed much. He missed Nam, but we don't hold that against him. He knew what he wanted and put his engineering degree to good use. We pulled the door closed and headed for the house.

Everyone gathered around the fireplace except Shirley and Katie who stayed in the kitchen and got the food ready. Candy's girls asked her to tell the story of the lady who wanted something from Avon. Candy's mother sold the stuff for years and when Candy came home her mother retired and gave her the route. "The floor's all yours," I said. "If the girls say this is a good story, then we'd like to hear it." Shouts went up from every corner. Even Uncle Leo whistled and Crank barked his approval.

"Well, my stories aren't as good as Grandpa's, but I'll give it a go if you guys are interested," Candy said. We assured her we were. Missy lowered the volume on the radio. We got comfortable and Candy began her tale.

"Some of you know I sell Avon to elderly women who live at Edge of the Woods apartments in the Soo. I met Miss Thelma last year. When I walked into the lobby someone yelled if I had any of that 'liquid deodorant.' I turned to see who belonged to the voice. Four old women sat on a couch, all in a row like birds on a telephone wire. The morning mail had not yet arrived and they were waiting for the postman. I asked who had shouted at me. Four index fingers pointed to a woman who had folded herself into the rocking chair to my right. She was all bones and red hair."

"Just like the old lady you used to tell us about, Jewel Red Nails, right?" asked Missy.

"Yes, Honey. She even looked like Jewel. Anyway, Miss Thelma wanted two bottles of the liquid deodorant."

"What's liquid deodorant?" Dotty asked. "Wouldn't it run down her armpits? And how would she put it on?"

"Your girls remind me of Ronnie," Squeaky said. "Remember how he always interrupted Grandpa? He was quite the character. Are he and Sara coming?"

As if on cue, Crank barked. Candy stopped telling her story as Sara and Ronnie opened the door. Sara was carrying their son, Hank, who was a holy terror. As his parents took off their boots and shook snow from their coats, Hank made a beeline for the twins who screeched with delight. The room was filled with conversation, carols, kids laughing and crying, blinking Christmas lights, and thanks to Shirley, the delicious aroma of a turkey. It had been a long time since the sideroad kids were together in one room. I looked around and was amazed at what I saw. Most of us had known each other since childhood. I never could have imagined the kids would have kids of their own, and we'd be together this Christmas.

"Mom, finish the story," Dotty said. "Skip all the other stuff and get to the good part when Miss Thelma told you she came home to die. Oops." Laughter filled the room as Dotty put her hand over her mouth. "I spoiled it," she said.

"Nonsense," Candy said. "It was just a silly story like Grandpa used to tell. It's not important. Who wants to sing Christmas carols? Uncle Leo, rosin your bow and get your fiddle going. Flint, warm up your harmonica. Elizabeth, the piano has your name on it. Squeaky, throw some birch on the fire. Let's get this party started." And that's what we did for the rest of the afternoon. By the time everyone had packed up and gone home, it was half-past ten. Uncle Leo had been in bed an hour, but I wasn't ready to call it a day. I poured a couple jiggers of brandy in a fancy glass, lit a cigar, sat in my chair, and watched the flames reach for the chimney. Suddenly I felt like an old, old man.

Today had stirred many memories. I was glad the laughter and talk kept most of them at bay. Squeaky's toddlers and Hank almost pulled down the tree as Candy's girls passed around plates of food and filled our coffee cups. After the meal, the women washed the dishes, the young ones fell asleep, and we men smoked the cigars Danny had brought. There wasn't time to think about Blew and Johnny. They were mentioned, of course, but only in passing. We didn't dwell on them or the hole they had left in our hearts. Today was a time for laughter and singing, but now that the room was quiet and I'm alone with my thoughts, I can't ignore the memories. If things had been different, Johnny, Blew, and me might be straddling the chrome chairs in the kitchen and making plans for the New Year. I wouldn't be sitting in Aunt Ida's easy chair, swilling Danny's expensive Hennessy and puffing on an even more expensive Cuban cigar. But things aren't different. They are the way they are. I'm alone, and my best friends are in that sleep from which nobody awakens.

It makes me furious when I think about what could have been. Johnny gave up before he was old enough to understand things always change. I learned that as a kid, but Johnny was soft. I'd known rejection all my life. I was a pro at handling it, but Johnny was still a kid. If he had learned patience as I had, he would have waited. Katie would have changed her mind. I'm certain of that. She means it when she says she'll never marry or have children. Johnny's more alive to her now than he was when he lived. He used to tell me that when she rode behind him on Butterball, her arms went around his waist and his heart beat so loud he thought she could hear it. Why'd you do it, Johnny? Why didn't you reach out to one of us? We'd have gotten you through that night and the next and all the nights that were to come. We were your pals.

I poured a little more booze into Aunt Ida's favorite glass. She didn't know brandy was supposed to be drunk from a snifter. Nobody in Chippewa County would have known that. We're farmers. We know about plowing and planting and harvesting, but not about certain glasses for certain drinks. Did the Vietnamese villagers know about such things? Hell, no. If they had clean water, they'd have drunk it from the boot of a dead soldier. Blew was in the construction engineers. I was in the 32nd Field Artillery Regiment stationed at Phu Loi base camp. We depended on the engineers to make roads through the brush. It was dry there. No rice paddies. We saw images we couldn't get out of our minds. Didn't have to be dead bodies. Just ordinary people trying to live ordinary lives in an anything but an ordinary war zone. Maybe the Vietnamese understood it. They were used to occupation and war, but none of it made sense to us boys.

I hate thinking about Nam. It was a total waste. When we got back on U.S. soil, nobody other than our parents welcomed us or shook our hands. That war changed teenagers who served because our country told us we had to. Danny was smart. He hid in Houghton, earned a degree, and didn't think any more of what was happening in Southeast Asia than we thought about what was happening on the campus of Michigan Tech. Maybe he was right. Maybe we were stupid. None of us returned home the same as we had left.

Well, I don't know. What'd you say, Crank? Would you go to war for no reason other than you were told to go by politicians? Of course not. Want out, boy? Don't stay out long. Do your business and get back here where it's warm. I opened the door and felt the slap of cold wind and wet snow on my face. Crank hesitated, but only for a second. The call of nature was stronger than the snowstorm. Uncle Leo hollered from his bedroom. He wanted water. Crank came back in. I turned on the tap and realized the pipes had frozen. Damn. That's one thing we never worried about in Nam. An average day was close to or over 100 degrees. Even in the hootches at base camp, the temp was in the 90s except at night when it got down to 60 or 70. I laugh when I remember how we complained about the cold. Good. I caught the freeze-up just in time. I'll leave a tap running during the night.

The lamp was on when I entered Uncle's room. "Here's your water," I said and handed him the glass. "Damn pipes almost froze. We've got to have a better setup next winter. Heat tape, maybe." I was about to leave when he asked me to take the chair in the corner and put it by the side of his bed. He looked old. His blue eyes were watery and surrounded by dark circles. His hair and mustache were white. His hands, once so strong and healthy, were now boney and crippled by arthritis. Flesh hung from his throat like the wattle of a rooster. "You okay?" I asked. "Wind keeping you awake?" He ignored my questions.

"We had a good day," he said. "I enjoyed myself. Thanks for including me in the fun. You're a good boy, Flint. I hope you learn to play the fiddle. When I'm gone, it'll be yours."

"I'm game, but you'll have to teach me. How'd you learn?" I was sure he'd start talking about the old days, and I wished I'd brought the bottle of brandy with me, but he didn't. His eyes got that faraway look, and I knew not to press him about the past. It held some pretty awful memories. "You want anything else?" I asked. He shook his head and set the water on the stand. "Goodnight, Uncle. See you in the morning." I tucked Aunt Ida's quilt underneath his chin and turned off the light. "Sleep well," I said. He didn't answer.

The fire had burned low in the grate, but I still wasn't ready for bed. There were times I didn't think I'd come back here if I survived Nam. There's a big wide world beyond this little peninsula we call home. After the war I traveled a bit, but whenever I tried to settle in one place, the call to return kept nagging me like a gal who wants to get married will nag a feller until he gives up and gives in. Those of us who were born here understand. This isn't a magical place. It doesn't have much to offer except acres of land and three of the Great Lakes. I thought about sailing on a freighter. I used to enjoy reading books about sailors and shipwrecks and ghosts haunting Davy Jones' locker, but when I took a long, hard look at what I really wanted, I knew it couldn't be found on the water. What I wanted was right here. Her name wasn't on a freighter, but tattooed on my arm—Candy. Maybe this coming year will be the one she marries me. I hope so. If not, if that no-good husband of hers comes sniffin' around and she takes up with him again, I'll be a bachelor. I remember old man Sims saying there was nothing better than being your own boss without having a woman poking her nose in and telling you everything you were doing was wrong. He and his buddy from Sugar Island said women were nothing but trouble. I didn't believe them then, and I still don't. A good woman—the right woman—is a treasure.

Katie

I suppose I was always a wannabe rebel in one way or another. As a child I was obedient. Even in my teenage years I never did anything that would cause my parents to be ashamed of me. I was a good Catholic girl. Unlike some of my classmates, no boy would have ever gotten me to "go all the way." Sometimes Mum would talk about a girl who "had" to get married. She always looked at me and smiled and said she was thankful she had no worries about me in that department.

Mum divided everything into departments. It was her way of keeping topics organized in a meticulous way. One department was for kitchen matters. Another for how to handle her in-laws. A third kept track of how much wine Grandpa consumed after the deaths of Granny and Jewel. I think the one she guarded the most was labeled "Katie's Dos and Don'ts." That's why I never told her I joined the SDS—Students for a Democratic Society—when I was at MSU. She would have been horrified. The SDS was my ticket out of the safe world of the sideroad.

Once Johnson announced he wasn't seeking a second term and RFK jumped in, we believed he would stop the insanity of Viet Nam. I became a student activist. My roommates considered me a proponent of what they called the "new left" whatever that meant. All I knew was I hated the war, wanted to vote for someone who would stop it, and firmly believed students should be active participants in government. That belief was not new. I had been politically outspoken since twelfth grade when I shocked Mrs. Hutton with my "radical" views that weren't radical at all except in our little town in the Eastern Upper Peninsula where high school students weren't expected to seriously discuss the Cuban affair, Khrushchev, the assassination of JFK, and all the other political stuff considered much too complicated for dumb hicks like us.

By the time I graduated from MSU, the SDS had splintered into various factions and I was done with it. I joined the Peace Corps despite Mum's absolute refusal to agree to my going. She worried where I would be sent and the potential physical danger I might be in. I said I didn't care. One country, one war was as good as another. The Corps was my ticket out of my claustrophobic existence. I was sent to Samaipata, a small village in east Bolivia where I lived with the locals and worked with other volunteers to improve sanitary conditions. The place was primitive but so beautiful I wanted to stay indefinitely. My parents had other ideas and when my two years were up they demanded I return home. I said goodbye to my friends and that was that.

By then any rebellious streak in me had been quelled, at least temporarily. Viet Nam raged. The Tet Offensive killed Russell and Danny's friend, Paul, from Paradise. MLK was dead. RFK was dead. People were burning their cities. The Chicago 7 were on trial. Herbert Humphrey was the best candidate the Democrats could put forth to run against Nixon. My God. What a mess. I spent most of my time alone in my room. I didn't want to see anyone. I wanted to forget what had happened the night of high school graduation, but I couldn't. The passage of time hadn't dulled the memories. They were still fresh and raw.

I don't know how I got through those first few weeks after Johnny's death. Of course I blamed myself for not giving him hope. I was so concerned about telling the truth it never occurred to me the truth might be the worst thing I could have said. It wouldn't have changed my plans for the fall. I still would have moved to East Lansing and attended Michigan State. Johnny knew that. He knew I'd be away until Christmas when I would have come home for a few weeks. I wouldn't have returned for Thanksgiving. He knew that, too, but insisted he'd drive down to see me which made me feel suffocated. It wasn't that I didn't care for him. I did. I loved him, but I wasn't *in love* with him. That was something he couldn't understand.

When Mum called and told me Blew had died, my roommate, Angel, comforted me as visions of Blew filled my mind. I saw him in his cap and gown, giving everyone a salute as he practiced for the Army. I saw him the day he boarded the plane that took him away from us. It was almost too much to bear. Angel understood. The previous week she had received word that her brother, Byron, was dead. He was a Marine and his head was blown off during a Viet Cong ambush near Dong Son.

Blew had survived Viet Nam. It didn't make sense he returned from war only to die in our river. Would people I loved never stop dying? It started with Johnny. I was furious when I heard what he had done. His suicide was meaningless. I told him I couldn't promise to be his wife. For Christ's sake, we were only eighteen. Our lives were ahead of us. Why didn't he understand I couldn't make a commitment on that night because secretly, the good girl he knew was a wannabe rebel.

* * *

I'll do it today, she said to the empty rooms. If he could leave me then so can I. It made a lot more sense than continuing the nightmare called life without her brother. She had no friends, no family now that Byron was gone. She decided to walk into the lake and simply disappear. Since childhood Angel had thought about dying. She used to play pretend and would grip her neck and pretend to choke herself. She had an imaginary lover she called Quinton (she had not yet read about Faulkner's Quinton) who would save her at the last minute. Bryon often teased her and asked why she didn't like life. She was pretty enough. Slim enough. Smart enough. Why wasn't she strong enough to endure the daily grind. Yes, the same genes passed from one generation to the next. The same problems with no solutions. War, poverty, disease. So what? Brother and sister knew, as did the whole of mankind, that such things would never end so why fly against them?

Lake Michigan was visible from their back porch. Waves, heavy with the chill of February, rolled underneath the ice that extended from the rocky shoreline. Among the rocks and discarded slabs of concrete, Angel gazed at ice crumpled into rough ridges like corrugated metal roofing. Jagged edges of white rose from the wreckage, reflected pale light that filtered through thick winter clouds and sharpened the cold, bone-dry air. She had no desire to return to this special place. She walked away from the water moving underneath the ice, walked towards the cottage Byron had bought for them, and absently gripped the doorknob.

The quiet of the foyer hit her first, slapped her like the icy wind she had left outside. Quiet squatted where there should have been voices. Quiet hid among her things and hung from the peg next to the Carhartt jacket Byron would never wear again. She buried her face in the material. She clung to his jacket, smelled the faint essence of his scent, and waited for some invisible strength to propel her deeper into the folds of the rooms. Something stirred inside her. Hope, maybe?

* * *

I suppose I was always a wannabe rebel. Maybe that's why my subconscious brought Angel's story to mind. She had told me over and over again she would never love anyone as much as she had loved her brother. She said that kind of love was too painful. She also tried to convince me life was better as a pagan. There were no ridiculous Christian rules to follow, only Samhain with its mysteries and strange celebrations. Samhain marked the Celtic New Year. It signaled the end of summer, the harvest season, and the beginning of winter. I was disgusted with the Catholic Church and Pope John XXIII who had thrown out the rules I had followed throughout my childhood and teenage years. I was tempted to attend the Samhain celebration until she said it was associated with death. I was tired of hearing of death. I wasn't interested in the Celts who believed the veil between the living and the dead was thin. Unlike Angel, I had no desire to be visited by spirits. If they had been capable of driving memories from my mind, I might have given paganism a try, but Angel didn't offer an opinion on the ability of spirits to eradicate memories.

Why do visions of the past haunt me? It's been years since I thought about Angel. Why now? Always questions with no answers. Grandpa used to try and explain things to me, but I couldn't grasp his words anymore than Johnny could grasp mine. It was a futile endeavor for Grandpa, but he never gave up. Even today he tries to help me understand life. He doesn't want to die with unanswered questions between us. The other day he invited me to join him on his daily walk to Jewel's cabin. We sat on the porch bench. The afternoon was warm. Robins called to their mates. Crows flew overhead. Rabbits hopped in the yard, occasionally stopping to feed on purple clover. Grandpa was silent for what seemed like a long time but might only have been minutes. Without turning to me he began talking.

"What God has set in motion, man cannot change," he said. "I want you to remember that. What I'm going to share with you isn't the ramblings of an old, senile man. It's the picture in my head I've never told anyone. I want to share it with you because you're so much like Jewel sometimes I can hardly stand it. The morning I married your Granny, loud caws of crows circled us like funeral wreaths. It was hot. Stifling for that time of year. As we spoke our vows that awful heat snuck in and out of the church like a thief. Mrs. Mansfield said the marriage should never have been. She said the heat was God's way of burning those who witnessed it, and it was our punishment for stealing that which belonged only to the matrimonial bed. I paid her no mind. People always say such things in a small town, but no matter, Katie, for some things are, whether or not they should be." Grandpa asked me if I knew what he meant. I said no.

"People give life to words. There were plenty of folks who said I shouldn't have married your Granny, but I wasn't one of them."

"Did you love her?" I asked. He got that peculiar look in his eyes like people do when their mind wanders or they're trying to think of something to say.

"Gladys floated down the aisle as if walking on a cloud. She carried a bouquet of daisies. Her dress was ivory colored. I remember the hem dragged on the floor and when the ceremony was over, it dragged on the dead, scorched grass when we left the church. She was pretty. Her cheeks were pink. She said it was the heat that colored them."

"Did you love her?" I asked again.

"It takes a long time to love someone," he said. Then he stopped talking. I knew it was time to tell him about the note I had found stuffed in a slit between my closet door and the wall.

"Grandpa," I said. "I found a note Granny wrote a long time ago. It's in my pocket. Do you want to hear what it says?"

"A note? What kind of note?"

"It tells a secret I don't think she wanted anyone to know. Do you want me to read it to you?" He shook his head.

"No, I don't think so. Your Granny was always writing notes. I find them everywhere. Most were lists."

"Not this one. It's about the day Mum was born." He sat up straighter.

"Where did you say you found it?"

"In a slit between the wall and my closet door."

"That used to be our room. Why do you have it in your pocket?"

"I carry it with me whenever we come to Jewel's cabin."

"You might as well read it. Her words can't hurt me now."

I took the envelope from my pocket and began to read. "It was the sound of wind shaking the shingles that awoke me that morning. That and the child I carried. She had been busy all night. Kicking and chasing herself in my womb as if to say I've been here long enough and I want out. It was that time of year when everything was covered with dust and you can't get ahead of it no matter how hard you try. July and so hot the baked earth would hardly grow weeds. I was in the field when my water broke. The flood couldn't seep into the hard ground. It lay in a puddle. I walked to the wagon and crawled in. I yelled to Clayton. He came running and carried me to the house. I was afraid he might drop me, but he was strong and patient. There was no time to call the midwife so he took her place. Eva was born in our bed. When Clayton held her, I knew he loved me. He wed me to protect my good name. He cared for Jewel, but she had Mrs. Mansfield, and I had no one. Now I have everything." Grandpa's eyes filled with tears. I asked if he had fathered Mum. He didn't respond. He just kept patting my hand and repeating how much I reminded him of Jewel.

We never mentioned that note again, and it doesn't matter who Mum's biological father was. Grandpa was her dad and had married Granny to save her honor and protect her from shame. Actually, nothing seemed to matter anymore. I hated the 1970s and their strobe lights and burned draft cards and 99 cents a gallon gasoline and the relentless Viet Cong who didn't know they were defeated but just kept coming, garbed in twigs and mud, too stupid and fearless to know they couldn't win a war against the Americans, but smart enough to know they couldn't lose it either. Every place I looked there was civil disobedience and body parts flying helter-skelter on the six o'clock news and remnants of Woodstock and drugs and women screaming about equal rights. I drifted through the seventies much as a grasshopper jumps from one blade of grass to another looking for something it can't find because it doesn't know what it's looking for.

"Katie, are you going to sit in that chair all day?" Mum asks, shaking me out of my reverie. "You're young. Do something with your life." She's holding a dishrag in one hand and a paring knife in the other. She's making a salad for supper. "I don't like to interfere, but you've got to get a job. We didn't pay for your college education so you could run off to some strange country and come back home and mope. Grandpa, tell your unhappy granddaughter it's time she got a job. What about teaching?"

"Oh, Mum, don't worry about me. Look at Candy. She made a mess of her life, but she's back on track. Flint wants to marry her and this time I think she'll say yes."

"So you want to get married is that what you're thinking? That another failed marriage will make you happy? What happened to you, Katie? You want to be like Candy? Is that your goal? I used to praise your intelligence, but now I don't know what to think." Mum's voice trails off as she turns her attention to cutting up cucumbers and tomatoes.

"No, I'll never marry again, you know that, Mum. I'll get a job, but not teaching. I'm waiting for a call from the editor of the paper. I think I'd make a good reporter." Mum grunts. I know what she's thinking because we have this conversation almost every day. She's disappointed I haven't found a cure for cancer or run for Congress. How do I tell her I've lost my way? That the last decade took everything out of me? That my husband was a good man I came to despise because I mistook his goodness for stupidity? That if I hadn't escaped, he would have suffocated me? How do I tell her I was glad we didn't have a child? All Mum wanted to be was a wife and mother. That's not my way. We're worlds apart. If I don't get the job I want, I'll have to move on because if I stay here much longer, I'll lose my sanity. Dad and Grandpa try to understand, but

Mum's convinced I'll never amount to anything. "I'm going to Candy's."

"Will you be home for supper?"

"I don't know."

"Well, the salad will be in the fridge if you want it. Watch out for deer and be home before dark. I love you."

"Love you, too, Mum." She hugs me. In her eyes, I'm eight years old.

Candy and her daughters live in an old farmhouse in Fibre. She rents from a relative of Flint's uncle. When she left Toby her mother was ashamed and after a few weeks told Candy it was time to find her own place. Flint convinced his uncle's friend she'd be a good renter, and she is. Her home is decorated in typical Candy style—charming, warm, and inviting. I pulled into her driveway and her girls ran to meet me.

"Guess what, Aunt Katie. Guess who's coming to see us?" They're jumping and shouting as if Jesus Himself is dropping by.

"I give up. Who's coming?"

"Daddy," they yell in unison. "Daddy's coming all the way from Mississippi. We can't wait." They grab my hands and propel me towards the house. Candy's shelling peas on the porch.

"What's going on?" I ask. "Is Toby actually driving north?" She nods.

"Why? What does he want? Did you invite him?" She gives me a look that would freeze water.

"Are you crazy? He phoned and said it was time he saw his daughters. I asked why. He's had no contact with them for over a year. Not even a birthday or Christmas card let alone a gift. I don't want him here, but my lawyer said there's nothing I can do to stop him. Legally, he has visiting rights. The girls are anxious to see him, but I'm dreading it."

"Have you told Flint?" She nods again.

"He said to play it cool and not lose my temper and to call him anytime I feel threatened."

"Do you?"

"No. Toby's not violent. He's just stupid."

"Don't call Daddy 'stupid'," Missy tells her mother. "I love him and he loves me. He said so on the phone."

"I'm sorry, Honey. Take Dotty and ride your bikes to Uncle Flint's. I'll call him when your Daddy arrives."

"No, I want to stay here." Missy pouts. "Just because you hate him is no reason why Dotty and I should."

"I don't hate your Daddy. Stay at Uncle Flint's for an hour. Aunt Katie and I want to talk."

"I know Uncle Flint wants to marry you, but he'll never be my Daddy. Only Daddy will be that. If you're going to talk mean about him, I'm going back with him and you can't stop me," Missy says.

"I'll help you pack."

"I hate you, Mama." These are Missy's parting words as she and Dotty pedal down the lane. I look at Candy. She doesn't seem bothered by her daughter's tirade.

"Well?" I ask.

"Well, what? Forget what she said. You know how it is. The parent who raises the kids is always the one who gets the blame for everything while the parent who is only a vapor is idolized. If Toby wants to take Missy, he's welcome to her. She's too much for me to handle. Before you eat all the peas, shell a few and throw them in the pot."

"Remember Blew's pea patch and the fun we had eating our fill as we picked them?"

"How could I forget? Remember the time we filled water pails with peas and lugged them down to the riverbank and the boys joined us? Remember how we took our time shelling them and eating one pea at a time and the boys ate like Johnny's pigs gobbling their food in the troughs? God, but those were the days. We were so young."

"I remember laughing so hard I peed my pants and was embarrassed until Blew said my pee had given up its ghost just like the nuns had told us Jesus give up His when He died. I was furious with him and said he couldn't compare pee with Jesus. Those were the days I believed everything the church told us. That's when Blew said there was no hell, no limbo, no purgatory, and the priests and nuns were liars. I remember him saying there probably wasn't even a heaven." Tears filled my eyes. "Oh, Candy, why did the boys die? Why did they leave us?" She hugs me.

"If I knew the answer to that, I'd probably know why I married that damn fool Southerner. I hate to admit it, but yesterday when he phoned and I heard his drawl, my knees went weak. After all these years, that jerk still has power over me. His voice was pure honey, drawing me in like a bee to a flower. What the hell will I do when I actually see him? I know he'll put his arms around me and kiss me hard."

"What do you want to do?"

"Nothing. I want him to leave and never come back."

"Then ignore him. He'll spend time with the girls and get the message."

"Sure, Katie. Sure, that's exactly what I'll do, maybe, but don't be surprised if I take a vacation and go back with him."

"You wouldn't, Candy. Please tell me you wouldn't do that. It would destroy Flint."

"Calm down. I didn't say I would. It's just a thought, that's all. Besides, you know Flint as well as I do. He can survive anything. That's the last of the peas. Come in and have a drink." And that's how we spent the rest of the afternoon. Candy with her bottle of gin and me with Mr. Daniels. We drank until we were almost drunk and then I left because that's what wannabe rebels always do. Return to the comfort of the familiar. But I didn't go home. I drove to a seasonal road and parked. I looked at the parched fields before me. The grass had been gone for weeks. There was no rain. I wanted to feel the cool green blades underneath my feet, not the brown ocean the field had become. I wanted to run barefoot on the hot ground until my feet burned. I opened the Mustang's door and took off my shoes and socks. I would run as fast and far as my feet would take me. I would run until every memory had been seared out of my body and departed through the soles of my feet. I would no longer be a wannabe anything. I would be a rebel and rejoice in the rebellion I had kept at bay since I was two years old and realized I was alive.

Shirley

2024

I am old now. Lines crisscross my face in no particular pattern as if some drunken spider forgot how to spin her web. But when I was young there were no lines on my face. They were hidden deep within my soul where daylight never touched them. I'm tired now, too. My twilight years are lonely as was my childhood until I ventured from the room above the kitchen where I played with my dolls. I loved them as a mother loves her children. As I wanted Mom to love me. She did, of course, in her own way, but I didn't recognize it until we became friends and moved away from all the memories holding us hostage. I lost her twenty-five years ago. Sometimes it seems like yesterday. Sometimes it was an eternity. I'm glad she didn't live to see the madman who was elected to the Oval Office in 2016. I'm glad that no matter what happens this year I won't live long enough to know if our democratic system will stand or fall. Katie and I often talk about the future. We're thankful we have no grandchildren.

Occasionally I write something in this, my online journal. I don't know why. Perhaps I think someday in the distant future a weary traveler will chance upon my musings and find them useful. I hope so. I haven't done much with my life. Do any of us? Was Shakespeare's Macbeth right? Is "Life but a walking shadow, a poor player that struts and frets his hour upon the stage and then is heard no more? Is it a tale told by an idiot, full of sound and fury signifying nothing?" I think I prefer the quote from "As You Like It" spoken by Jaques in his Seven Ages of Man speech: "All the world's a stage and all the men and women merely players. They have their exits and their entrances, and one man in his time plays many parts." We all do that, don't we?

1958

Every night I had the same dream. It frightened me to the point where I dreaded going to bed and would often talk to my brother, Squeaky, who was in his room on the other side of the wall. He would tell me to go to sleep and when I did, this is what I saw: *Gray kittens everywhere, little open mouths covering tiny faces, crying for help that did not come. Suffocating darkness enclosing burning hot August sun. Running, flinging aside white screen doors, searching empty houses. Blue Easter eggs growing eyes, cracking, crying. Jesus hanging on a chocolate cross, blowing bubbles through a yellow straw. A brown rubber boot. A rosary. A black-robed priest. Coffin dropping, disappearing, down, down, far from my reach. Gray closed eyes, gray sky, gray face grazed by ice. Black veils. Purple light shining through stained glass church windows. Barbed wire necklace, ripping flesh. Blood everywhere. Broken Horn bawling.*

I would awaken when I heard the cow bawling. In the distance, as if miles and miles away, as if in heaven or some other faraway, unknown place, I would hear Mom's voice. She would tell me to wake up, but I couldn't. I wanted her to hold me, but she wouldn't so I kept my eyes closed and pretended I was asleep. After a few minutes she would leave my room. That's when the nightmare returned, but I wasn't sleeping. I was going over and over what I remembered of my sister's funeral. I saw her lying on a granite slab, only there wasn't any granite just a coffin lined with pink satin where the undertaker had put MayBeth after dressing her in a new pink outfit as if she were going to church. She even wore lacy white gloves. Her hair was combed and arranged around her face so that curls framed her cheeks giving her the appearance of a China doll in a Wards Christmas catalog. After my conscious mind saw her, the nightmare would return. *Funeral director wheeling coffin to altar. Wheels slapping on church floor. Suckers growing hands, clapping, cheering, opening wide mouths. Red nails pulling from the hands of Christ. Running, heading for woods behind the barn and the river behind the woods. River silently gathering strength, pulling crying newborns under until they were silenced by brown water. Screams.*

That's when I usually awakened, but I didn't cry out or whimper so Mom never heard me. I longed to tell her I needed her, but I didn't because that's the way it was in our family. We never told each other anything of importance. We talked about the weather and getting hay in before the rain came, but we never talked about what was in our hearts. Maybe we were silent on that front because if we had told each other how we felt, how we really, truly felt, we wouldn't have been able to face each other and that would have been worse than keeping quiet. Maybe all families were like ours. I didn't know then, and I don't know now.

Some nights when I dreamed of MayBeth, she surrounded my bed. Sometimes we walked to the kitchen. I would see the honey-stained cupboards, the cracked pitcher that held our kitchen utensils, the box full of white birch waiting to be put in the stove, the white table with the stained yellow oilcloth covering its wooden plank top, the yellow granite pails that held the drinking water, the washstand where we scrubbed our faces every morning. I would see clay pots of green ivy circling the kitchen windows and clean yellow curtains hanging stiffly from their rods like soldiers in a line. I would smell smoke from the woodstove and freshly baked white bread as Gram took it from the oven. I saw her slicing thick chunks for MayBeth and me. She always dipped her knife into the butter bowl, scooped some out, slathered it across the heel of the hot bread. We watched it melt into the crust. Then she would leave the kitchen and float through the rooms, through the upstairs, touching her old iron bed, her fairytale books, her shoes, her dog, Sparky, as he waited patiently on her bed, waited patiently for her return.

1961

The night Goldie freshened the weather was cold and crisp. I remember the barn was quiet because the cows were sleeping and the radio had long since signed off. Occasionally the silence was broken by the scurry of a mouse as it ran from its hiding place and looked for food in the cats' dish. Sometimes Goldie's moans broke the silence. She was unlucky because she usually had a deformed calf and Pap had to shoot it. That's why we were anxious about this birth. The waiting was hard. Earlier in the evening Pap had called the vet. I was at the barn when he arrived. He didn't hold out much hope for either Goldie or her calf. He said the birth would probably be breech like last year. He told Pap to have his rifle ready. That was when Pap told him to go home. He was old and his job exceeded his knowledge, but what did I know? Pap said he'd let nature take its course and hope for the best. I believed him.

It was late and Mom told me to go back to the house, but I didn't. I stood outside the door and imagined what thoughts were passing through Goldie's mind. Words came to me as clearly as if Goldie had put them in my ears. I imagined her thinking that she didn't know where the pain ended and her calf began. I didn't know anything about the birthing process, but I thought there must come a point when there's no difference between the pain of being born and the pain of dying. Pap opened the door and broke into my thoughts. He said he knew I hadn't gone to the house. He came out to make sure I was okay.

He lit a Camel cigarette and the smell of lighter fluid and puffs of smoke filled the air. He pointed to the Big Dipper but said he didn't know the names of other constellations. I knew his schooling ended in third grade when winter came and his feet could no longer bear the cold ground as he walked to school. He had no shoes, let alone boots. He was nine years old. When his Pa died a year later, Pap inherited the only thing of value—a pair of black boots with no patches. Gram lost the farm that spring and moved Pap and his sisters from place to place. They lived as vagabonds. He didn't tell me this. Gram did. When Pap finished his smoke, we went back in the barn.

Mom finally agreed it was okay if I stayed a little longer so I sat on a bale of straw next to Gram who was sleeping. I saw Mom rest her head on Pap's shoulder, and I remember thinking that if love could be measured by touch or glance or motion, it still would have remained measureless in the barn that night. I remember hearing Pap say it was time. Mom told me to turn away and I did. I didn't see the calf being born, but I saw it wobble to its feet. It was a healthy little heifer. I watched Goldie lick her baby, and I cried tears of thankfulness along with Mom and Gram. When Pap was certain all was well, he turned off the light, and we stepped into the night. The walk to the house was joyful.

The fire had burned out in the kitchen stove and although the room was cold, we didn't feel it. After hanging our barn jackets in the back shed and taking off our boots, Pap stirred a few coals to life, got a flame going, and added kindling and dry wood to the stove. It wasn't long before the chill left the kitchen. Mom made hot chocolate for me and tea for her and Gram and Pap. Then she warmed cinnamon rolls Gram had baked earlier in the day.

We sat around the table and talked. That was the first and only time I was in the barn when a calf was born. Pap said it was no place for a young lady. He was a good man but like others of his generation, he struggled to understand his role as husband and father. Because he brought his wife home to his mother, he was caught between two strong-willed women but that night there was no bickering, only the peace that comes after a long, hard battle.

While growing up, I don't think I showed Pap how much I loved him. I took him for granted because he was always there. Never once did I pay for gas when I filled the gas tank. I stopped at Osborn's gas station on old US-2 and charged it to his account. Even when I backed the car out of the garage and concentrated so hard on not going in the ditch I hit the side of the garage, Pap only laughed. Then there was the time I visited a friend and was pretty sure I couldn't clear the distance between the car and the tree but tried anyway and crumpled the fender. Pap saw the humor in it. My last driving mishap occurred when I was twenty-one. I pulled into the garage and didn't leave enough room on the passenger's side. I ran to the house crying that I couldn't get the car to move because it had scraped the right side of the garage and was stuck. Pap laughed and said it might be time to marry me off and let my husband do the driving.

Over the years, I learned men show love for their daughters in different ways. In my case, it wasn't with words but with actions. That night so long ago was one I remembered as the sweetest of my childhood because I knew my Pap loved me.

1965

Pap committed Mom to the Newberry State Hospital after I graduated high school. Her depression was so bad, he felt he had no choice. She was there almost ten months. I put my plans to attend college on hold and took care of the cooking and housekeeping. Gram was crippled with rheumatism but helped as much as she could. Squeaky left the sideroad and got a job on Mackinac Island. He was in no hurry to be drafted and sent to Viet Nam. Pap quit farming and started working at the Soo Locks. I was genuinely happy. I missed Mom, of course, but I knew she was in a place that might help her. For the time being Squeaky was safe, not like some of the boys we knew who had come home from the war in body bags. Pap had a good job, and we had hope for the first time in a long time.

And we were right. When Mom returned to us, she was a different person. She hugged everyone and said the house looked nice. It was clean and smelled good. She walked through each room, inspecting it as if she had seen it for the first time. Pap had installed plumbing, something Mom never thought she would ever see in our house. We had a real bathroom and a kitchen sink just like other people. I think she was overwhelmed by the changes she had begged and pleaded for throughout my childhood and teen years. The look she gave Pap was one I had never before seen. It must have been love.

I had dusted her piano and put a white crocheted runner on top of it. Gram had picked wild flowers and put them in the pink vase Pap had bought for Mom as a homecoming present. She sat on the piano stool and lifted the cover where eighty-eight keys lay in anticipation. She began playing her favorite piece, Pachelbel's Canon in D major. The music drifted throughout the house, filling the rooms with a sweetness usually reserved for a field of fragrant clover. When she finished playing, we waited and wondered what she would do next. Pound the keys with her fists? Slam down the cover? Scream at us to leave her alone? Cry? But she did none of these once-common behaviors. She turned, smiled, and said the house would hear her music every day if we agreed. Naturally, we said *yes*. She opened her arms and I ran to them. Pap stood in the doorway until she motioned him to join us. Gram hobbled behind the piano stool and put her arms around Mom's thin shoulders.

That moment of epiphany brought us closer than we had ever been. Mom was home and she was well and nothing else mattered. We moved to the kitchen where I had prepared a light lunch. Gram made tea and served it in our best china cups. We talked, we laughed, and we shed tears of gratitude. Things stayed that way for a year. Then a letter of acceptance and notification of a scholarship came for me. Madonna College in Livonia, a city south of the Mackinac Bridge and almost three-hundred miles from home, was looking forward to my attendance in September. When I told Pap, he was worried it might upset Mom, but it didn't. Gram said it was a good omen. I was determined to go. I knew if I missed this opportunity, I would never leave the sideroad.

I had applied to Madonna because I was interested in and intrigued by the Catholic Church. When our neighbor, Sara Odell, made her First Communion the summer of 1958 I was invited to attend the ceremony. Mom didn't want me to go because we were Protestant, but for the first time in my life, I disobeyed her. Mrs. Odell said I could ride to the church with her family, but I went with Katie instead. We were best friends. When I saw Sara in her white dress and veil, I thought she was beautiful. All the girls were dressed in white, and the boys wore white shirts, little black bow ties, and black slacks. The children looked like angels, even the boys. They were pious and clasped miniature prayer books between their palms. A rosary was draped over their hands. Everything was perfect—the kids, the nuns who followed them down the aisle, the white marble altar decorated with white flowers. That's when my longing to learn more about the Catholic faith began. It seemed so pure, I immediately decided I would convert to Catholicism, become a nun, and spend the rest of my life in prayer and service to God. When Madonna accepted me, I was thrilled.

However, it didn't take long for the thrill to wear off. I quickly learned that nuns were no different from anyone else. They were like the teachers I had in school. They were jealous of each other. I was on the student paper. If I wrote an article about the nun who taught art and it was shorter than the article I wrote about the nun who taught English Lit, I heard grumbling and complaining from the one who felt short-changed. They didn't even try to hide their disappointment or disgust. I was stunned these so-called "brides of Christ" were nothing more than petty women hiding underneath their habits and their beads. Take away their costumes, and their humanity—with all its warts and shortcomings—was plainly visible.

1968

When Katie called and told me Martin Luther King, Jr. had been assassinated, I couldn't believe it. I had listened to his speech the previous night and was awed by his words. They seemed so prophetic, almost as if he knew his time on earth was short. Katie was deeply involved in politics and had been since our high school years when she followed in her parents' footsteps and became a member of the Democratic Party. The murder of JFK had hit her hard. We were so young and felt so helpless, but Katie was determined to make a difference. She had always been a bit of a rebel, but I don't think anyone recognized the signs except me because I felt the same way. We were trapped by our environment. Our small town didn't encourage young people to be active participants in the democratic process.

Then when RFK was killed, Katie was devastated. She had planned on joining others and touring the country, knocking on doors, and getting out the vote. Once President Johnson announced he wouldn't seek another term, she devoted more time to campaigning than to her studies. It was the last week of classes at MSU, and she was packed and ready to leave with other students who believed Bobby Kennedy would stop the war that seemed such a waste of young lives. I called her and listened as she cried. She was as lost as the rest of us who believed he would have made a magnificent president. Katie returned home and married the first airman she dated. Three months was all it took from their first dance at the Northview Lounge on Portage Avenue in the Soo to their wedding at the Catholic church in Brimley. Three months.

17 May 69
Tam Ky, Viet Nam

Dear Shirley,

What I'm writing, you have to promise not to share with anyone. I gotta get it off my chest or I'll explode. You're the only friend I trust to keep quiet about it. If Daisy or my grandparents knew, they'd be scared to death.

Last night six of us were almost shot by our own guards. It was dark and when we approached the gate we were challenged until we convinced the guards we weren't the enemy. Folks back home have no idea how easy it is to get killed here by what's called friendly fire. It's part of war. Everybody has trigger happy nerves. The other day I was on watch with another soldier. His legs were hit by one of our own. Blood was everywhere. He was screaming as medics carried him out and loaded him on a copter that would take him to the nearest field hospital. I can't get the sight of his bloody body out of my mind. I'll never know if he died enroute or if he'll have to face the rest of his life in a wheelchair.

As construction engineers, we build and repair roads in lots of places. We have five bases where we're subjected to ambush, road mines, mortars, and sniper fire. It's no wonder our guys shoot first. It's either that or wait to be shot. We're in constant fear of threats all day, and it's worse at night so you can see why our men thought we might be the Cong. A few days ago, I was riding shotgun in one of the convoys. Before I knew what was happening and could do anything to prevent it, I saw the driver's head explode. Two other times we were sideswiped by another company of our own. I was horrified but we were lucky. They fired their weapons in the air and when they heard us yelling to hold fire, we were okay.

Accidents happen all the time on the roads we travel in convoys. It never stops. I've seen and done things I'm ashamed of and know I'll have to live with the guilt and shame for the rest of my life. Like the rest of the young guys here, I didn't know what the Army expected us to do to the South Vietnamese. Often innocent civilians are killed by mistake. Sometimes even on purpose to send a message if any are harboring the Cong. We pretend the carnage we see doesn't bother us. We're taught from childhood that a man doesn't cry, that we have to buck-up and do the job the government is paying us to do, but it's awful hard to ignore what went on in My Lai before we got here and what continues in Dong Tam, Long Binh junction, and other places. Now I know why men who fight in wars never talk about what they've seen. The homefolks couldn't take it. Nobody mentions suffering from shell-shock like the guys in the first world war, but whatever it's called now, the sound of mortar rounds and exploding grenades is horrible.

Thanks for listening, Shirley. I know I can trust you. I feel a little better. Burn this letter after you read it. Thanks. *Blew*

1970

Madonna was a good college, and I learned to tread carefully when dealing with the nuns. I stuck it out and graduated with honors. The nuns had tried to shield us from the horrors of what was going on in America with political assassinations, social unrest, the burning of Detroit and Cicero, and other major U.S. cities, and, of course, the Women's Lib movement and Southeast Asia. I wasn't interested in Gloria Steinem. She could keep her "Ms." magazine and all that went with it. My concern wasn't whether a man held a door open for me. My concern was the war. I desperately wanted it to end before all the I boys I knew had been killed. And I wanted a career, not just some dead-end typing job that paid the rent.

I didn't stick around for the formal graduation. I picked up my diploma and moved from my pleasant dorm room on the Livonia campus to a drafty loft on Monroe Street in Trappers Alley in downtown Detroit and set about looking for work. I wanted something exciting that would keep my mind off things I didn't want to remember or be reminded of. I refused to think about home and my obligation to my parents. Pap had paid for whatever my scholarship didn't cover and always sent pocket money which I was grateful for, but I couldn't stand the thought of moving back to Brimley and a dead-end life. I didn't have any friends, not real ones anyway. Not like the kids on the sideroad, but I knew the years would have changed them like they had changed me. Life is static only for stone statues. I called Katie's mother to get her address. She was somewhere in South America with the Peace Corps. Mrs. Clark said Katie had become a lost soul after graduating from MSU and refused to settle down. She divorced her husband after five months of marriage and left the U.S.

1975

Sometimes we end up doing the thing we dreaded most. That's what happened to me. I had vowed I would never get a secretarial job, but that's what I did. Not because I wanted to but because I wasn't qualified to do anything else. I had majored in History of the Ancient World but lacked a teaching certificate so I didn't belong in a classroom. And truthfully, I didn't want to teach ancient history. Nobody in their right mind would have the slightest interest in something as boring and dead as that. Maybe a handful of anthropologists, but they had their own books and didn't need anything I might offer, little as it might be. It would have been an exercise in futility. Why did I pick such an odd subject when I knew there was no demand for it? Maybe because I had spent so long reading about the past, that studying the ancient world was a way of escaping the present one.

Anyway, I was a good typist and I was smart and could get a job anywhere. That's how I landed in the law office of Potts, Potts, & Potts. The boys were triplets and bachelors. It was obvious to me they would rather have hired a male to do their typing, but one wasn't available so they brought me in. I think they were a little afraid of me. I had morphed from a shy country girl into a bristly modern woman thanks to the example of the nuns. If ever there was a rebellious, violent, angry group of individuals, it had to be the nuns I was in daily contact with for four years. I'm not saying they epitomized all nuns, only the ones I was acquainted with.

Billy Potts was the senior partner. He hated real estate law but that's what he was saddled with. His real ambition was to join the circus the next time it came to Highland Park. Buddy Potts was the second eldest. Wills and divorces fell to him. He loved the stuff that came his way. His secret ambition was to be the male equivalent of Ann Landers. Drawing up wills and divvying up money, homes, chattel, and children in a divorce proceeding suited him to perfection for it gave him an immense amount of data from which to draw upon should he ever have the courage to quit the partnership, or at least work on a parttime basis, and devote the rest of his day to the "Just Ask Buddy" column he planned to write. Willy Potts was the baby. He was given legal briefs that didn't require much expertise because his brothers considered him somewhat dimwitted. Apparently, his mother thought she was going to birth twins and had called it quits before anyone realized Willy was about to make an appearance, not on the bed, but on the floor of the bathroom, if not actually in the toilet, as he shot down the birth canal when Mrs. Potts was relieving herself.

While the country was struggling to recover from the Nixon fiasco, and Steinem and her crew were continuing to march for rights I thought women already had, and boys who had run to

Canada to avoid going to war were returning home, I was busy passing the time on the 21st floor of the Penobscot Building in downtown Detroit. My routine never wavered. Every morning I awoke at six a.m., practiced Transcendental Meditation for exactly twenty minutes, showered, dressed, ate one-half of a grapefruit, one slice of toast, and drank one cup of hot coffee, brushed my hair and teeth, and applied makeup. Then I walked from my loft to the office. Along the way, I admired everything—the cars and city buses whizzing past, the cops on horseback, the cracks in the sidewalks, the slivers of grass forcing their way through the cracks, other Detroiters as they sat on park benches or roller-bladed around me, drunks in various stages of inebriation and wakefulness, the amazingly beautiful windows of Winkleman's, Hudson's, and Crowley's. I noticed everything which made for an incredibly interesting morning walk. At exactly 8:58 a.m., I sat at my desk, uncovered my IBM Selectric, and got to work. At exactly 4:58 p.m., I tidied up my desk, covered my typewriter, and walked home. This was my routine for years.

I had saved enough money to quit my job and travel. Only problem was, I had spent so much time working, I had left no time for friends. My weekends had been whiled away at shopping malls and occasionally prowling the grounds of Madonna College. There was a long, low building on the property that had always intrigued me. Its doors were locked and the windows were caked with dirt and grime, but when I was a student and bored to distraction, I often left my dorm room and walked to that deserted building. I convinced myself it contained the bones of nuns who had been killed by their fellow sisters who were jealous of them. Naturally, I had no proof of such crimes ever having been committed, but lack of evidence didn't stop me from forming an iron-clad theory much as politicians do. Anyway, I was a creature of habit and walked the deserted grounds much as a ghost might walk through the halls of a home that had slipped from its hands. At least once every two months I could be found prowling where I had no business to prowl. Although I did not own a vehicle, I did have a driver's license thanks to the Drivers' Training program offered at the school in Brimley, and thanks to Willy Potts I also had access to a broccoli-colored Chevy Chevelle. I loathed the color, but I loved the car. Loved it so much I neglected to return it one sunny Sunday afternoon when instead of driving to Livonia, I headed north on I-75 and didn't stop to think about what I was doing until the Mackinac Bridge came into sight. By then, it was too late in the day to turn around so like all good crooks, I kept going.

If there was one thing admirable about me it was my determination to keep going. Growing up the way we did, my brother and I didn't have enough sense to quit. We were like that ridiculous pink bunny that advertises a battery. I don't remember whether it's Duracell or some other brand, and the name isn't important. It's the message that counts. Squeaky and I knew if we ever quit, that'd be the end of us. Maybe we were too stupid to know when to slow down. Maybe there were a hundred reasons why we kept putting one foot in front of the other until we'd gone as far as possible and then we decided it might not be a bad idea to take a break. Anyway, the Chevelle purred along as I crossed the bridge, got off the freeway, and turned west on M-28. I was heading straight for home.

That's where I was heading, but it wasn't where I ended up. I sailed past the sideroad before I realized it was behind me. I had forgotten how dark everything is in the Upper Peninsula once the sun leaves the sky. I turned by the blinking light that led to the main street of Brimley, drove through the town, and pulled into the casino parking lot on Lakeshore Drive. I'd never gambled in my life, but then again, I'd never stolen a car before either. If the triplets could see me now, I think they would have been proud of me for finally doing something unexpected. Billy and Buddy were always after me to *do* something with my life. Well, I had *done* something and figured I'd better call Willy and tell him where I was and that his car was safe. I stepped into King's Club and asked the first person I saw if there was a phone I could borrow. I was told to try the one at the bar. As I approached it, I was in for a surprise. The barmaid was none other than Candy. I nearly fainted when I saw her, and she nearly dropped the drink she was serving when she saw me.

We had decades worth of catching up to do and, obviously, it couldn't be done while she was working. After the initial shock, we hugged. I played the slots and lost more money than I made in a week, but I had fun. Being in King's Club was like being in Las Vegas. At least I thought so. The bright lights of the machines. The noise. The sound of coins dropping in the trough when someone got lucky. The laughter or moans, the cheers of winners and the groans of losers—I loved all of it. When Candy's shift ended at midnight and I had lost a lot of money, I still wasn't ready to leave, but she linked her arm in mine and practically dragged me out the door.

Instead of going home, we walked to the edge of Lake Superior and sat on a blanket she had taken from her car. It was a perfect night for memories. The full moon shining down on two girls huddled together as if they were children, the waves gently lapping the shoreline, an occasional call of a Canadian loon, everything brought memories rushing back to the days when we were kids gathered around a campfire. We talked until we ran out of words. Then we sat quietly until we had gathered more memories to rehash, and then we were quiet again until more images were resurrected from the past. It was late, or more accurately it was early in the morning of a bright new day, when we finally felt the cold that had burrowed into our bones. We arose and walked to our cars, promising to get in touch later that day, but we didn't. I don't know why, but when I turned down the lane leading to the old homestead, I didn't want to see anyone except my family. There would be time to make the rounds and visit all the kids who now had kids of their own. Candy must have felt the same way because she didn't call, either.

1979

When I called Willy and explained I hadn't actually stolen his Chevelle, I had only borrowed it, he laughed. That was the beginning of our love affair. He flew north, met my parents, and demanded I drive him to every little town in the Upper Peninsula until I had driven as far as we could go without having to rent a boat when we reached the Keweenaw Peninsula. Willy had never been anywhere. He lived with his brothers in the house his father had purchased in Grosse Pointe Woods. They cared for their ailing parents. Willy was thrilled to leave the mausoleum as he referred to his palatial home. He said my absconding with his vehicle was the best news he had ever received. It was a reason to board a plane and leave the city. He gave his siblings some lame excuse about my parents needing me and me needing him and said he'd be back when he got there and that I wouldn't return at all. I don't know what else he told them, but they were mad enough to threaten disbarment, although on what grounds was a mystery.

After seeing all there was to see in the U.P., Willy flew back to Detroit, but instead of telling his brothers he had returned, he took a job with the Wayne County Legal Aid Services. He rented the top floor of a warehouse on Bethune Street in uptown Detroit. I joined him a week later and started working as his assistant. We were happy. Willy was generous, friendly, obedient, and gifted with a marvelous sense of humor. We attended every art gallery opening, every opera, every concert held at Ford Auditorium, and amassed a group of wonderful friends. Artists, musicians, writers, leather-workers, and bums were among the many who gathered around our table almost every evening. People who had no money and no place to go showed up at our door. Within a few months of moving to Bethune, we became known as the couple who would help anyone, anytime of the day or night.

Willy blossomed during the first years of his new life. He gained self-confidence. He took on a persona Billy and Buddy would never have recognized. One I'm sure they would have rejected. Willy wasn't interested in making money. He had a trust fund he could draw from whenever he needed money for a client's bail or reliable transportation for one of our friends. He never said *no*. His wallet was never closed to any down-and-outer. Our years at Bethune were some of my happiest, but I was ready to move on. I wanted a house of my own. One with a yard. One in the suburbs that Willy hated. We knew our parting had arrived. As a final gift for the freedom I had given him, he handed me a check that, if I was careful, would last through the remainder of my life.

With some of the money, I purchased a small cottage in Wyandotte, a Polish downriver community. Then I went home. Pap had passed away a year earlier. I knew it was time to visit Mom, maybe even see if I could convince her to leave the farm and live with me. Other than her dog, Spider, there were no animals to tend to and no reason I could see why she wouldn't want to move or at least have an extended visit. Squeaky had moved Rachel into the house when they married. It was going to be a temporary residence until they saved enough money to buy a bigger and better home, but the longer they stayed the more they saw the potential the place had. After their twins were born, they abandoned all notions of leaving. Squeaky wanted to buy the half he knew would come to me upon the death of our parents, but I told him he could have the house and all the acreage free and clear. I never planned on moving back to the sideroad. When Pap died, I quit-claimed my interest so there would never be any question as to the legal owner.

Instead of farming, Squeaky planted spruce trees. Thousands of them at various intervals to be sold as Christmas trees. To sustain his family while the trees grew, he worked at the Soo Locks as a laborer and saved as much as possible. I was proud of my brother and Rachel. They were well-matched. For the first twenty years of our lives, I wished I could be more like him and be satisfied with my lot, but no dice. I'd always been a bit of an oddball. I have no doubt my personality could be traced to my childhood. When I wasn't playing with my dolls, I was reading every book I could get my hands on while Squeaky was playing with the kids. I devoured the Little Golden Classics, then moved on to Nancy Drew and books written by Mary Stolz. As a teenager, I was introduced to Dickens and Hardy and Austin and other English masters and felt I had found Utopia. Squeaky wasn't much of a reader unless it was comic books, but that changed when he met Rachel. He read whatever she recommended. At an early age, he was smitten and never looked at another girl. Even when he was in the service, he was faithful to her. I've never been faithful to any man and have no intention of starting now. Should someone come along I find interesting, I might give him a few years, but only with the understanding that I'm a free agent.

When I suggested Mom live with me, she was thrilled. I couldn't believe it. Mom leave the old homestead? Leave the sideroad? It didn't seem possible, but it was. Within a week, we had packed everything she wanted to take and were heading south. Spider loved every minute of the drive. We stopped when we thought he needed a break. We stopped when we wanted to see some sight of interest. We stopped for lunch when Mom spied a billboard that advertised a restaurant whose name caught her fancy. We stopped for no other reason than to stretch our legs at every rest area. We were in no hurry. I wanted her to enjoy the ride in case the final destination wasn't as exciting as the drive. She had never crossed the Mackinac Bridge or been any farther south than Pickford, twenty miles from the sideroad, so everything was interesting to her. As the miles sped by, I hoped her new life would suit her. We couldn't pack her piano, but I promised to buy her one as soon as we were settled.

After a nine-hour drive, I opened the door to my cottage. Mom couldn't have been more thrilled. By the second day we had her bedroom looking like something found in a French mansion, and she was ready to shop for a piano. We were lucky. I picked up a local newspaper and saw one for sale. It was a baby grand located on Grosse Ile. I called the number and within an hour, we were on our way. Within two hours, Mom was the proud owner of a beautiful baby grand Steinway. I made arrangements to have it delivered. Then I took her shopping at the local store that sold sheet music. When the grand arrived, the change in Mom was nothing short of miraculous. I finally had the mother I had longed for. Not since the death of MayBeth had I seen her so happy and lighthearted. Her music filled our rooms as well as our hearts. Life had never been better.

Perhaps if I had tried a little harder, I would have found Mom many years ago. She was always within reach. I just didn't know it.

1982

We were sitting on the deck overlooking the back yard and admiring our roses when Mom started talking about her fondest memories as a child. She said she loved to awaken early during the summers of her youth. Sunlight poured through the window in the bedroom she shared with her two sisters who were much older than she. The three girls slept in one bed. Mom was usually in the middle, but in the summertime she pleaded to sleep on the side closest to the open window. Her sisters agreed only after she promised to wash all the milk utensils. Robins calling to each other awakened her at 4:30. It was too early to get up so she would lie quietly, pretending she was asleep when her sisters arose at 5:00. They crawled over her. Once they dressed and ran downstairs, Mom looked out the window and watched the mist rising from the pasture. She loved the sound of the lead cow's bell as she led the way to the gate where they waited for her Pa to open it and begin the milking.

When her sisters married and left home, Mom had the bed to herself, but the routine that began in her childhood stayed the same. Every summer morning she heard her grandmother calling to her Pa. She'd sing his name from the bottom of the stairs, and he would answer that he was awake. Mom would hear him lumber out of bed. She said he was a large man, not so much in weight as in height. The springs of his bed would creak and groan as he heaved himself up and out. She listened as he tramped down the stairs and opened the door to the kitchen. Often the smell of coffee perking drifted up to her room. By the time Mom was thirteen, her mother had died. She missed her terribly, but the aroma of coffee made her feel that all was well. It wasn't, of course, because things are never the same when your mother dies, but Mom forced herself to believe that as long as she could hold on to a treasured memory, she would survive.

She said that when she finally dressed and left her bedroom, she joined her Pa at the barn. Most of the milking would already be done. She would sit on a bale of hay and watch her father as he rested his head against the flank of a cow. He rarely spoke unless it was about the weather. They never mentioned her mother or what impact her death had on them. Things like that weren't discussed in the old days. People went on as best they could. When the last cow had been milked and put out to pasture, Mom helped muck the stalls and put chop in their feed boxes. Then she washed the utensils and gathered eggs from the chicken coop. She returned to the house, ate breakfast, washed the dishes, and asked if she was needed for anything else. If the answer was *no* she returned to her room and put on one of her mother's dresses and her pair of high heels. She said how wonderful it was to feel her mother's presence when she borrowed her clothes. For a few minutes, everything in her world was normal and good.

1985

Katie's letter arrived today. She must be having a terrible time. It's hard for me to believe that the girl I thought had such a wonderful childhood and teen years could be so unhappy as an adult. She's been angry for years. I pity her. I've asked her to visit Mom and me and stay as long as she wants. We have a guest room, but she won't come. Today she wrote that every politician she's ever met is crooked including the one she used to work for. She said the lies get bigger and more dangerous the higher up the political ladder they go, and the common man on the street can't muster up the courage to demand an accounting. She considers Ronnie Reagan a threat to democracy. She says he's only an actor who reads his lines. No more. No less.

Her bitterness isn't camouflaged. She says Ronnie's wife is a bigger joke than her husband. While she's busy organizing her War on Drugs, he's busy telling the CIA to ignore the planes bringing them into our country. Why else would her war amount to nothing? Katie saw the drug culture firsthand. For all I know, she might have participated in it. She says we're fast becoming a nation of clones. She closed her letter by saying that echoes from the past fill her mind, chasing away rainbows, and locking her in a dark state of dysfunction and confusion. She asked if I thought she would ever be able to move on or would she forever be held hostage to the past. How am I supposed to respond to that? I came to terms with my own demons long ago. I don't want to sound cruel, but if she doesn't do the same, she'll wallow in heartache and regrets until the day she dies.

1993

Mom and I watched as the Branch Davidians burned. For days we were glued to the television wondering what would happen if Koresh didn't surrender. We knew he wouldn't. He thought he was Christ incarnate. Attorney General Janet Reno was out of her depth. Even President Clinton had no idea what to do. Maybe they should have asked Mom. She would have told them what she often told me—that most Americans had lost their common sense. It was the glue that kept us united. That made us strong and honorable until Reagan and his trickle-down economics made us a nation of fragments. Mom wondered if anyone even knew what a trickle was. She did. She knew it wasn't much, and anyone who believed he'd get wealthy from a trickle was only fooling himself.

The times were upsetting her. Nobody seemed satisfied with their lot. Men turned to men. Women to women. They exchanged their natural desire for the opposite sex. We couldn't listen to the radio because we never knew when a song with filthy lyrics would come on. People stopped going to church. She worried what toll the crazy behavior of adults was having on the young. She felt our country was in need of help. That somebody should send an SOS, but she didn't know where it should be sent. What country could help ours? Weren't we the greatest? Weren't we supposed to be a beacon to democracies all over the world? One evening as we sat opposite each other in our favorite chairs she looked at me and asked if I could hear the death rattle rolling across America. She said she could, and it frightened her.

2000

New Year's Eve 1999 came and went without any of the dire predictions of computers crashing and the grid being brought down. Mom insisted I fill the bathtubs, which I did, not as much to give her reassurance as to settle my own nerves. We celebrated the arrival of the new millennium with cups of tea and chocolate-covered wafers. Squeaky had called and wished us a Happy New Year and said they would be grandparents for the third time come July. Mom was thrilled to be a great-grandmother again. Holly, Squeaky's daughter, had married right out of high school and was expecting again. If ever a girl was cut out to be a mother, it was Holly. She had a sweet and gentle nature. Everyone loved her. I promised Mom we would visit the little newcomer in August which would give everyone time to adjust to him or her. Neither Holly nor her husband, Mikko—one of the Koski boys from Rudyard— wanted to know what they were getting. Mom set to work knitting booties and blankets with the same gusto she still summoned when she played her piano.

As for me, I was satisfied to putter in my flower gardens and tutor children in ancient history. I was even writing a book about a world I had failed to discover in my academic studies. It was great fun creating something from nothing but my imagination. My days were filled with excitement and pleasure, especially when Willy bought the cottage next to mine. We had kept in touch and when he retired and I mentioned the place was for sale, he snapped it up. He even accompanied Mom and me when we traveled north to meet Sally, the baby girl Holly named in honor of Blew's mother. She knew the stories of the sideroad kids as well as we did.

The years passed as years are wont to do. Sometimes I still dreamed about MayBeth. The dream was always the same and never scary, or maybe I was no longer frightened by anything my subconscious dredged up. I could feel a cool hand gently stroking my forehead. It could have been my hand or my sister's or even Mom's. Once I thought it was God's. Whoever or whatever was touching me, loved me, that was obvious. Even in my sleep, I could feel the tension leaving my body, replaced by a peaceful, loving spirit. It was like a blanket of grace enfolding me. Occasionally I heard a voice as sweet as honey, as soft as a kitten, and as gentle as a warm summer breeze. I could feel strong arms surrounding me. Without the slightest hesitation, I would lean into them and plan what MayBeth and I would do. The plan was always identical. *We would take the rowboat out on the river and see if we could catch something other than suckers. Then we'd pick the last of the peas and eat until we almost burst, and then we'd run up the hill, run all the way home. On the clean kitchen counter there'd be fresh bread waiting for us and lots of yellow butter and red strawberry jam. In the middle of the kitchen table, goldenrod would be standing in a pretty glass vase and tiny bugs would be scratching their heads, wondering where in the world they were and how in the world they got there. We'd climb the ladder to the haymow and dangle our legs over the edge and watch the cows eat away the last of the summer grass. We'd talk about God and whether or not He was real, and we'd agree it didn't matter because some questions have no answers.*

In my dream, that's what we would do, and the day would fade away and before we knew it, another day would come to take its place until another day pushed it out of the way, and then another day would come, and another and another until all the todays ran out, and we would run into the tomorrows. As much as the dream of my childhood frightened me, this one calmed me. When I visit Squeaky and we talk about the past, we remember it with fondness that only time can bring because it dulls the pain of reality. We weren't neglected or ill-treated. We simply were lonely for our parents. Although we lived in the same house, we each kept to our individual corners. Sometimes now when I look at Mom, she smiles as if she knows what I'm thinking. It's an unspoken bond we probably always had, but I, like my brother, was too young to be aware of it.

I'm looking forward to the new millennium and what thrilling things it will bring. I'll finish my book and self-publish it. That's all the rage now. Willy is adamant about covering the costs. He practically lives at our cottage. Who knows? Maybe one day I'll agree to marry him. Wouldn't that be a hoot? I'd insist on being wed on the land of my youth with all the sideroad kids and their kids and grandkids in attendance. I can almost hear Elizabeth saying, "What! You want kids at your wedding? You want children as your attendants? You want to exchange vows in a tent instead of a church? You country people sure have peculiar ways." But most of all, I picture MayBeth and Gram and Pap and the little brother Mom lost and her favorite Hereford, Broken Horn, and Johnny and Blew and Grandpa and Jewel Red Nails and all the others that left us—I picture them gathered together, watching me as I, the girl no one understood, said vows I waited a long time to say. Now, wouldn't that be a hoot?

About the Author

Sharon M. Kennedy lives in Michigan's Upper Peninsula on the land of her youth. As an opinion writer for Gannett Media, her newspaper columns reflect a keen observation of people and their experiences. Whether humorous, serious, or poignant, she records events and situations relatable to individuals of various ages. Kennedy has the remarkable ability to communicate with readers as if they were sitting at  her kitchen table, sharing a cup of coffee and a laugh with her.

The Adventure Begins Here!

The SideRoad Kids follows a group of boys and girls as they enter the sixth grade in a small town in Michigan's Upper Peninsula during 1957 - 58. This meandering collection of loosely-connected short stories is often humorous, poignant, and sometimes mysterious. Laugh as the kids argue over Halloween treats handed out in Brimley. Recall Dorothy's Hamburgers in Sault Ste. Marie. Follow a Sugar Island snowshoe trail as the kids look for Christmas trees. Wonder what strange blue smoke at Dollar Settlement signifies. Discover the magic hidden in April snowflakes. Although told by the kids, adults will remember their own childhood as they read about Flint, Candy, Squeaky, Katie, and their friends.

"Katie, Blew, Squeaky, and Daisy grew up on farms instead of high rises and used their imagination instead of fancy gadgets to make their own fun. An entertaining read for youngsters. And parents, you might enjoy a nostalgic flashback as well. I know I did."

—Allia Zobel-Nolan, author of *Cat Confessions*

"The stories in *The SideRoad Kids* are often humorous. However, underlying them is a sensitive awareness that being a kid, rural or urban, then or now, is not easy. This is an enjoyable read that will enlighten today's kids about the past and rekindle memories for older readers."

—Jon C. Stott, author of *Paul Bunyan in Michigan*

"Sharon's stories capture the essence of childhood and growing up in a small community. The antics of The SideRoad Kids will keep you entertained and take you back to a simpler time."

—Renee Glass, Senior Production Artist, *Mackinac Journal*

Learn more at www.AuthorSharonKennedy.com

From Modern History Press

Enjoy U.P. Stories from the View of a Yooper

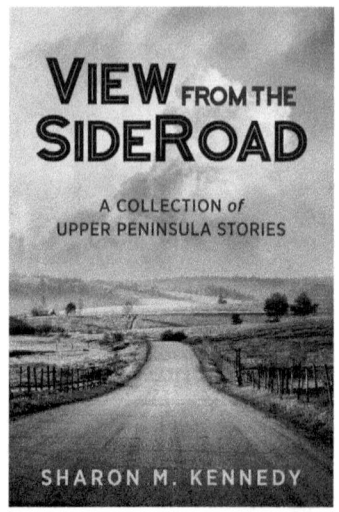

Join us for a trip through Michigan's rural Upper Peninsula in this collection of fictional short stories. Let the characters of *View from the SideRoad* surprise you with their resilience, humor, and unpredictability. Whether it's a sailor who shuns water, an old maid who wants to shoot her cats, or a man who keeps his lover in the junk drawer, the stories range from witty to wry to weepy. Sharon is a master of the short form. As readers of her newspaper column and previous collections will attest, she never disappoints. Her stories will keep you turning the pages and thirsting for more.

"Penned by Sharon Kennedy, a hidden gem in the wilds of Michigan's Eastern Upper Peninsula, this book is a fine collection of humorous, satirical, and poignant stories."
—Jim Dwyer, Contributor, *Mackinac Journal*

"*View from the SideRoad* weaves vivid tales with warmth and humor. The author really knows how to captivate the reader with tantalizing stories."
—Jill Lowe Brumwell, Author of *Drummond Island: History, Folklore, and Early People*

"Sharon Kennedy is one of the Upper Peninsula's premier writers. A well-read columnist in the Eastern U.P., she has turned her attention to writing books and U.P. literature is the better for it. Her stories are reminiscent of Cully Gage's, *Northwoods Readers*, but with her own spin and style."
—Mikel Classen, Author of *True Tales: Forgotten History of Michigan's Upper Peninsula*, recipient of Charles Follo Award

Learn more at www.AuthorSharonKennedy.com
From Modern History Press

www.ingramcontent.com/pod-product-compliance
Lightning Source LLC
Chambersburg PA
CBHW051839020726
47502CB00005B/1862